CHILDRENS

HIT

Please renew or return items by the date
shown on your receipt

www.hertsdirect.org/libraries

Renewals and
enquiries: 0300 123 4049

Textphone for hearing   0300 123 4041
or speech impaired

Hertfordshire

FROG AND THE SANDSPIDERS OF ARIDIAN

FROG AND THE SANDSPIDERS OF ARIDIAN

Joffre White

Book Guild Publishing
Sussex, England

First published in Great Britain in 2012 by
The Book Guild Ltd
Pavilion View
19 New Road
Brighton, BN1 1UF

Typesetting in Century Schoolbook by
Nat-Type, Cheshire

Printed and Bound in Great Britain by
CPI Group (UK) Ltd, Croydon, CR0 4YY

A catalogue record for this book is available from
The British Library.

ISBN 978 1 84624 766 8

For Simpkins with all my love

Prologue

The Second Dimension ...

A lifeless desert landscape stretches out into distant horizons; only the dark featureless shapes of sand dunes fill its panorama. Two large, silver moons hang in a star-peppered sky, illuminating the scene with an eerie, pale grey light.

In a small hollow, a dust devil stirs and slowly rotates, picking up granules of sand, spiralling them higher and higher, twisting itself into a column which grows to over 2 metres in height. The speed of the wind increases. Flickers of lightning crackle and sparkle within the churning cyclone as a figure begins to form and shape itself. The features that develop are that of a robed woman, her fair hair cascading down around her shoulders, her young face both beautiful and wicked. Her skin is as pale as the moonlight.

With one loud, explosive burst, the wind stops and the loose dust and sand falls to the ground around her. As she looks up at the twin moons, she raises an arm and a wand appears in her outstretched hand. She

1

stabs the black, twisted wand into the ghostly coloured sand and an evil, cruel smile spreads across her face.

'Free. Free at last. Now I shall have my revenge,' she shouts into the night.

Below ground, a great cavern is bathed in a warm blue light; its source is numerous glowing crystal rocks placed on stone plinths, which encircle a stone altar set at the cavern's centre. Upon the altar there sits a sacred Rune Stone. Shadows reach up high into the intricately carved ceiling and play with the delicate patterns. The light shines on four life-size statues of two men and two women that look down on the scene. The detail of their individual attire differs from statue to statue, except for the hooded robes draped over their shoulders; their stone faces stare out, stern and solemn.

A lone, cloaked figure stands before the altar; a hood conceals the head and face of the wearer. The pale, almost translucent Rune Stone begins to glisten and shimmer from a light of its own making. It rises and floats unsteadily, its vibrations sending out ripples through the air.

Two arms stretch out from the cloak. Golden bangles adorn each exposed wrist, decorated with the Magic symbols and runes belonging to a Guardian of the Dimensions. Slowly, the bangles are brought together and a bright, white streak of plasma snakes out and forms a blue orb around the now juddering Rune Stone.

A woman's soft, calm voice speaks from within the hood.

'It will not be that easy for you to take, even though I

2

alone cannot hold back the vile destruction that you bring with you. For the moment, I have sealed the Rune Stone beyond your influence. I do not know how you came to Aridian, but I pledge that I shall do everything in my power to safeguard this world and the security of the Four Dimensions.'

The figure turns, raising her arms even higher, static lightning streaking out from her wrists to connect with the stone statues, whose eyes flash open.

Her voice comes again, stronger and more insistent.

'I call upon my fellow Guardians. The dark threat to the Dimensions has returned. Aridian is now the battleground. We must join the circle once again. We need the Chosen One. We need to recall the legend that is Frog.'

1

Caught in the Act

Our World ...

it was a dark Friday afternoon in late February. Chris Casey had finished all of his homework and was about to reacquaint himself with the world of the Internet. It had been a while since he had been allowed the privilege.

He had worked hard at school during the winter months, earning enough merits to achieve his platinum award and badge, but it had been tough; the first month or so after the previous year's summer break had been a disaster. He had returned from the holidays with an excess of energy and the inability to concentrate on his work and subjects. His consistent chattering to his class friends about any topic, school related or otherwise, had interfered with his own and their education. His teachers were driven to distraction by his antics and it had finally been necessary for one of them to write no less than three warning entries in his journal in the space of two weeks. One more entry and he would be introduced to the experience of a full detention session: something he had never needed to fear because of his previous high standards of work and good behaviour.

As understanding as she was, his mother had been dismayed and had firmly explained that if there was another report of unruly conduct, written or otherwise, then all of his after-school activities would be withdrawn, including his beloved Taekwondo and his street dance club.

He could only put his reckless and excessive behaviour down to the disappearance and loss of his father some months previously. He still found it hard to deal with his absence and his thirteenth birthday in September had been a particularly sad occasion without his dad's presence.

The fantastic adventures that he had experienced during his summer break had given him some diversion. However, he felt that he couldn't share what had happened with anyone, even with his best friend Billy Smart, and so it seemed that his release valve was to keep talking about anything else that he could think of.

Finally, being faced with the prospect of losing all after-school activities and being totally grounded (weekday evenings and weekends), he had reasoned with himself one night as he lay in bed.

'What would Frog do?' he had asked himself and from the recess of his mind a familiar voice from his past adventure had echoed, '*He'd do the right thing.*'

That night he dreamt of dragons; of riding on their backs through moonlit clouds and feeling the fresh wind rush though his hair. He heard their enchanting voices fill his mind with calm and reasoning.

The next morning he had gone back to school with a renewed focus and determination. Over the weeks before and after the festive season, he steadily gained commendations and merits until he had achieved the top grades in his class and received a brilliant beginning-of-year report.

So, after weeks of hard work, here he was, being rewarded for his efforts. His mum had finally given him access to her precious computer. The homepage of Google stared him in the face and he did something that he had always wanted to do. His friends had told him of a thing called 'Ego Surfing'. It was when you typed in your own name and saw what information and links came up on the Internet. He slowly entered his full name, Christopher Norman Casey. He pressed the search button and watched as the screen blinked and then went blank!

He hit the enter key several times, then the escape key, but to no avail. The flat, grey screen just stared back at him. He was about to press the power switch and reboot the computer when the screen turned a shimmering silver and he watched, transfixed, as a familiar shape appeared on the screen.

'You've got to be kidding me,' he gasped. 'It's my flag. Frog's flag.'

Staring back at him was a white pennant with the image of a leaping green frog on it.

How could this be on the Internet? he wondered.

Curiously, he hit the enter button again and the image faded only to be replaced by a message which scrolled across the screen.

'Belzeera has returned.
The Dimensions are threatened once again.
We are in need of the legend that is Frog.
Cassaria, Guardian of Aridian.'

Chris gathered his thoughts and then tentatively typed into the keyboard.

'What do you want me to do?'

He pressed enter and waited until a new message appeared.

'Make haste to Aridian.
Use the sword to travel the Slipstream.
To open the passage to this Dimension
its blade must be plunged into free sand.'

Chris typed his response.

'How do I know that this is not a trick?'

A reply quickly appeared on the screen.

'A message from your old friend Gizmo –
Remember young Frog, not
everything is as it seems.'

Chris raised a smile as he typed in his reply.

'I'll be there as soon as I can.'

The screen faded and with another blink, the Google homepage reappeared. The printer came to life and Chris watched in amazement as an image of the leaping green frog slid into the tray. He picked up the piece of paper and stared at it as the memories came flooding back of his adventures in Castellion and the friends that he had left behind. He pictured their faces and he recalled his promise that should they ever need him again he would cross the Dimensions to help.

As he sat there, thoughts and images filling his head, Tabby wandered into the room and brushed against his leg. He looked down and absently stroked the cat.

'Looks like the Internet will have to wait,' he said as a familiar tingling feeling ran across his forehead and a soft golden glow filled the room.

He got up and went to the bathroom and, looking into the mirror, he saw that the mark of the Chosen, the sign of a golden burning sun, had reappeared on his brow.

'I hope this isn't permanent or I've got a lot of explaining to do,' he sighed.

He need not have worried; as he stood running the message over in his mind, the glow receded and the sign faded. He looked at his watch: 17.20. If he was going to make his move, it had to be now.

Learning from his previous visit, he went to his bedroom and emptied his pockets, making sure not to take anything with him that could present a danger. Then, he made his way downstairs to the kitchen where his mum was sitting at the table. She was attempting the latest Sudoku puzzle in the daily paper.

He stood in the doorway and took a moment to study her features. Although she was still the same strong and caring person, he had seen a difference in her since the loss of his father. A spark, a brightness, in her personality was missing. Friends would call and encourage her to go out with them, to socialise, but she would gracefully decline their offers, choosing her own company and immersing herself in her love of historical novels, or throwing herself into research work for the library where she was head librarian.

One day soon, he thought, *I'll share my adventures with you.* He then made his way across the kitchen and said, 'Hi Mum.'

She looked up. 'Where are you going, young man?'

'I'm just going out to the shed to fetch something,' he explained.

'What's wrong with the computer? You haven't crashed it have you?' she asked suspiciously.

'No, it's okay. I just need to get something from the shed, that's all.'

'What on earth would you want to bring in from the shed?'

'I've got some old toys in a box out there and I thought that I might clean them up for you to sell at a car boot sale.' His intentions were true, just not at this moment.

She eyed him for a second and then she said, 'All right, but don't be long. Tea will be ready at six o'clock.'

'Sure,' he replied as he disappeared out of the door.

'And don't get dirty,' she shouted after him.

'Of course I won't,' he replied and added, 'I love you, Mum.'

She smiled to herself warmly and then continued with her puzzle.

Outside, Chris opened the door of the shed and felt for the light switch. He flicked it with his finger and the old 60-watt bulb glimmered into life, illuminating the interior with a greyish light, which struggled to push back the dark shadows. He stepped inside, closing the door behind him and looked around at the various gardening and DIY equipment. A workbench stood to one side and he turned to face the old chest of drawers opposite. He hadn't opened it since the day that he had returned from Castellion nearly seven months before.

Taking in a deep breath, he knelt down and slowly pulled the bottom drawer open. He moved aside some old toys and reached further back to find the cloth bundle and the small wooden box just where he had left them. With trembling hands, he brought them out and placed them onto the floor. He slowly unwrapped the bundle and stared for a moment at the medieval clothes, the short sword in its scabbard, the dragon-skin waistcoat and the coiled whip. Old memories spun again in his head.

Picking up the box, he examined the strange runes that decorated its surface and marvelled at the absence of hinges or any visible means of opening it. He then slowly brought the box closer to him and whispered, 'Frog.'

As he said the word, the top melted open to reveal a crystal glass whistle and a long silver chain. He felt along the chain to find the unseen talisman and as soon as his fingers closed around it, his hand turned transparent. The Magic worked its way up his arm, beginning to turn his entire body invisible, but he let go, allowing his arm to return to normal.

'Just checking,' he said, as if to reassure himself, then looped the chain around his neck.

Ten minutes later, he had changed into his 'Frog' clothes. The green hooded cloak embraced him like a long lost friend. He placed the glass whistle in the leather pouch, which hung on his belt along with his sword in its scabbard. The leather whip was coiled, bandoleer style, across his chest. His normal clothes were now bundled up and placed inside the closed drawer.

He moved to the far end of the shed and pulled back a pile of plastic sacks that covered a small, unused bag of builder's sand.

'Right, I'd better get on with it I suppose,' he said purposefully as he drew his sword and plunged it into the top of the bag. Nothing happened. He pulled out the blade and tried again. Still nothing. He stood there for a while, running the words from the computer screen through his head. Finally, with a smile, he carefully withdrew the sword and sheathed it. Grabbing hold of the bag, he dragged it to the door and out around the side of the shed. A small trail of sand following him. In the dark gloom of the chilly evening, he tore it open and poured the contents onto the ground.

'That should do it,' he smiled. 'That is unless you're the wrong sort of sand.'

He drew his sword again and this time he could see that the blade was shimmering with a blue and white light.

'That's more like it,' he said and checked his watch: 17.45. 'Aridian, here I come,' he added as he thrust the sword into the pile of sand.

Suddenly, a pair of arms wrapped around him from behind, the hands clasped on top of his hands, making it impossible for him to release the sword.

'Gotcha!' said a familiar voice in his ear.

Chris turned his head sideways and shouted in his assailant's face.

'Not now, Billy. Not now!' But he knew that it was already too late as the Slipstream opened up and they fell forwards, spiralling into the swirling galaxy of spinning stars and flashing lights.

It was night-time and the air was chill. The boy who was now Frog found himself sitting on the top of what appeared to be a large sand dune. Stretching out to the horizon was a vast desert with what looked like a craggy rock formation far away in the distance. Two silver moons hovered unnaturally large and close to the horizon and the sky was filled with a blanket of bright shimmering stars. He tilted his head back, taking in the thousands of scattered diamonds twinkling in the dark velvet backdrop.

'I should have known that you would be here,' he said. 'You seem to follow me everywhere.' Sure enough, hovering high above him, was the familiar shape of Orion's Belt and he thought back to that evening in July when he had been looking up at the same formation of stars from his bedroom window and his adventures had first begun.

A groan by his side caught his attention and he looked down at the semi-conscious figure of Billy Smart sprawled out on the sand.

'This is going to be interesting,' said Frog getting to his feet. 'What the heck am I going to do with you, my friend?'

Billy slowly opened his eyes. 'What happened?' he groaned.

'Well, it's a good job that we're not going anywhere at the moment, because it's a long story,' said Frog as he helped his friend to sit up.

Billy blinked his eyes and squinted to take in his surroundings.

'Why are there two moons and where did all this sand come from?' he asked, turning to Frog. 'And why are you dressed like that?'

'I'll answer all of your questions if you promise not to freak out on me,' said Frog.

'Why would I freak out on you?' said Billy.

'Because even with your vivid imagination, this is going to be too weird for you, so you're going to have to pay attention to what I say,' answered Frog.

Billy slowly got to his feet and turned around; he looked out at the desert, which stretched away in every direction, fading into the dim horizon. He bent down and picked up a handful of sand, slowly letting it run away through his fingers, and then he turned and stared straight into Frog's eyes.

Frog stared back. Billy was the larger of them by at least fifteen centimetres. He had a stocky build with broad shoulders and a round, pleasant, freckled face framed by thick fair hair. It was now that Frog noticed Billy was wearing his hooded jacket and combat trousers.

Billy was just younger than him by two months, but he had already mapped out his future.

'When I grow up,' he had announced on numerous occasions, 'I'm gonna be a drummer in a rock and roll band. Either that,' he would sometimes add, 'or I'm gonna invent something really amazing.'

In the meantime, he was just a fresh-faced thirteen-year-old who, in Frog's opinion, was the best mate anyone could wish for.

'Are you listening to me?' Billy's voice jolted Frog's thoughts back to their present situation. 'We were in your garden,' he continued. 'I grabbed you; we fell into a hole of swirling lights. I saw weird shooting stars and then I got really dizzy and everything went black. Now I wake up miles from anywhere in the middle of a cold desert at night with not one, but two moons in the sky and you're dressed like Robin Hood.' He took a deep breath. 'I think that you've already got my attention.'

'There's a lot to tell you, Billy, but as I'm not sure exactly where we are I think that we had better start moving. We can talk while we walk. Besides, moving about will warm us up,' he said.

'Okay, Sherlock Holmes, which way do you want us to go?' Billy asked.

'There seems to be a sort of orange glow coming from those rocky shapes in the distance. I guess that way's as good as any,' said Frog. 'If we follow the ridge of this sand dune we can at least keep watch around us.'

'What for?' asked Billy.

'I'm not sure, but I think someone will turn up eventually,' replied Frog.

Just then, as if on cue, a low wail echoed out across the landscape.

'Or some*thing*,' added Billy looking around cautiously.

Frog instinctively drew his sword and on seeing the blade glint in the moonlight, Billy took a step back.

'Wow!' he exclaimed. 'Is that for real?'

'Yes,' said Frog. 'It's what seems to get me into and out of trouble.' He took a cautious look around them. 'Come on,' he continued. 'Let's get moving.'

2

Friend or Foe?

As they shuffled along, Frog told Billy about what had happened to him during the summer holidays, starting with the discovery of the suit of armour in his garden, which turned out to be Sir Peacealot, and what the Slipstream was and how time practically stood still between the Dimensions and home. He explained how he had inherited his new name and that for some reason his real name was not to be used in the Dimensions. He described Castellion, the friends (and enemies) that he had made, the journey through the Labyrinth, the battle with Lord Maelstrom and Fangmaster and finally what he was doing when Billy suddenly appeared and grabbed him in his garden. To emphasise the point, he rolled back his sleeve and showed Billy his watch. It was stuck at 17.45.

Billy had listened intently to every word that Frog said, interspersing it with 'Wow,' and 'No way,' on several occasions.

After a few seconds of silence, Billy spoke.

'Do you mean to say that we could be here for days and our parents wouldn't even know that we're missing?'

'Not just days,' replied Frog. 'Weeks or even months.'

Billy breathed out with a whistle. 'Neat,' he said.

'Aren't you worried?' asked Frog.

'About what?' replied Billy.

'Well,' said Frog. 'You've been transported through time and space into another world and Dimension. I don't exactly know what this place is or what danger we may be in. I don't even know when or how we'll get back home.'

'Look,' said Billy with a smile on his face. 'Our parents don't know that we've gone, time is standing still at home and by the looks of things, I won't be going to school tomorrow and if this is going to be anything like your last adventure I might even get to fight some bad guys. This is brilliant. Why should I be worried?'

Frog opened his mouth to encourage Billy to exercise caution, but then he closed it again, knowing that he would be wasting his breath. Things didn't generally frighten Billy and he had always been quite daring. He would always stand up to bullies and although he could be stubborn and a little reckless, above all, he was a good and loyal friend.

They journeyed steadily on and Frog enlightened Billy with more details concerning his previous adventure. Billy was particularly impressed when Frog pointed out his now visibly shortened little finger and how he had come to lose the end of the digit at the hands of the wicked wolf leader, Fangmaster.

Billy could not contain himself. 'Can I touch it?'

'Sure,' said Frog. 'It doesn't hurt, just tingles now and again, particularly if I get near a dog.'

'It's weird that no one can see it back home,' said Billy, examining the stump with macabre glee.

'I guess that it's all part of the Magic of the Slipstream,' said Frog.

They had gradually been descending from the ridge and the sand had flattened out beneath them when Billy suddenly stopped and looked down at his feet.

'What's the matter?' asked Frog.

'I think that I've stepped in something squishy,' answered Billy inspecting his trainer. 'Oh! That's gross,' he said, holding his hand out as far as he could.

'Don't move,' ordered Frog.

'What is it?' asked Billy.

'I'm not sure, but there are tracks all around us, lots of them. I would say that whatever made them is pretty big.' He knelt down to inspect the dark shape that Billy had stepped in, noticing several other dark piles in the same area.

'What is it?' Billy asked again impatiently.

'Well, it could be a lot of creatures with big feet, or a big creature with lots of feet. Either way, I think that you've trodden in its droppings,' said Frog with a smile.

Billy looked at his dark, stained hand in horror. 'Oh, Pooo!' he exclaimed.

'Exactly,' replied Frog.

'This isn't funny,' complained Billy. 'How am I going to clean this off?'

'In the absence of water I would suggest that you use some sand to rub off as much as you can. But do me a favour Billy.'

'What?'

'Stand down wind; you're starting to whiff a bit.'

18

'Right! That's it!' shouted Billy. 'I'm going to use you as a toilet roll.' He lunged towards him and Frog twisted away at the last moment sending Billy rolling in the sand.

'You're for it now,' said Billy and then he was on his feet and after Frog, chasing him out across the sand.

Frog was keeping a good distance between himself and the enraged Billy when he suddenly lost his footing. He turned as he fell and found himself on his back, staring up at the stars. He had underestimated how fast Billy was moving, because before he could get himself back up, Billy was on him. He straddled himself across Frog's chest and pinned his arms down with his knees.

'Let's see how this mixes with your hair,' he said gleefully as he raised his soiled hand in the air above Frog's face. Before he could carry out his threat, however, he was struck still and even in the pale light, Frog could see the colour drain from his face. He was transfixed, his eyes wide open, staring in wonder and in fear, and then Frog began to hear the low, menacing hiss come from behind him. Sensing danger, he thought back to the battle training that he had received on Castellion. He threw Billy to one side and rolled in the opposite direction, drawing his sword as he sprang to his feet. What greeted him made him step back, more in surprise than fear. Towering over them, no more than a couple of metres away, was a gigantic, hairy black spider. Its dark eyes stared out at Frog and a hissing, almost wheezing, sound was escaping from its partly open mouth, which revealed a pair of ivory white fangs.

Frog ran over to the now kneeling Billy and stood in

19

front of him. He raised his sword, ready to defend them both, but knowing in his heart that the odds were not good.

'Stay that sword,' commanded a voice and the spider lowered itself forwards in a crouch to reveal a white robed rider. His clothing was Bedouin in style and a cloth headdress masked his face. He held a small crossbow in his hands. The bowstring was taut and loaded with an arrow aimed directly at Frog's head. Frog slowly lowered his sword and sheathed it, and then he put both of his hands in the air.

'That's better,' said the voice. 'Tell your friend to do the same.'

Frog turned to Billy. 'Get up and put your hands in the air,' he said. 'And be careful; this isn't a game,' he warned.

As Billy got to his feet, another giant spider silently appeared beside the first. Its rider was dressed similarly, but his robes were sand coloured and as he dismounted, the material seemed to merge with the surrounding landscape, taking on the same hues as the sand and making it difficult to see him. As he approached Frog and Billy, the other rider kept his crossbow aimed at Frog.

'What do you want?' asked Frog.

'I don't think that you are in a position to ask questions,' the man snapped. 'Now turn around and put your hands behind your backs.'

Frog and Billy did as they were told and the man very quickly tied their hands and blindfolded them.

'Hey, what's going on?' he heard Billy complain. 'Chris? Are you okay?' he asked.

'It's Frog. I told you that my name in the Dimensions is Frog,' he said.

'Okay, okay! Frog. Are you all right?' Billy asked.

Before Frog could answer, a voice spoke very close to his ear.

'So, you say that you are the one known as Frog? If this is true then our mistress will be very pleased. She has been waiting for you. We were told to look out for one boy, but never mind; we can always feed your friend to the Sandspiders if he is of no use to her.'

'Not the sort of adventure that I was expecting,' said Billy.

'I did warn you,' replied Frog.

'Enough,' said the voice. 'No more talking from now on; you just do as we tell you.'

Frog was guided forwards until he could sense a strong, musty smell. This was then replaced by a wave of hot, rancid breath that washed over him and caught in the back of his throat. He was aware that the spider was inches away from him, taking in his scent until it let out a low hiss.

He heard Billy exclaim. 'Oh! This is really gross.'

Next, hands were lifting him up and he found himself sitting in the surprisingly soft hair of the giant spider. He felt the man sit down behind him and his arms reached around Frog. There was a half-whistle, half-hissing noise and Frog felt a lurch as the great beast lifted itself up. Another jolt and they were moving quickly in a rocking motion as the drum of the spider's feet passed over the sand. He could only hope that Billy was not far behind on the other spider.

After a while, they came to a halt and Frog could hear other voices.

'What have you got there?' asked one.

'Fresh meat for your spider's breakfast?' laughed another.

'Maybe, but we must take them to be questioned first,' replied the rider. 'Open the doors.'

There was a grinding, rumbling sound and then the spider lurched forwards again. The atmosphere changed instantly and there was a slight echo to the spider's movements. Frog could sense that they were no longer above ground and their motion was downwards, travelling along some sort of passage.

Soon, the air became stronger with the spider's musty odour. With another half-whistle, half-whisper from the man, the spider stopped and Frog felt it lowering its body. The man slid away and then Frog felt hands reach up and pull him down to the hard and unyielding ground beneath his feet. His blindfold was removed and he found himself staring at a pair of deep, green eyes; the rest of the man's face was still masked by the Bedouin-style cloth scarf.

'Stay there,' commanded the man and he turned back towards one of the spiders.

Frog took in his surroundings. They were in an enormous cavern, which was bathed in a bluish light; its source was the strange crystal rocks placed around the walls. On each side were large gated stalls; some of them were occupied by more of the giant spiders, and Frog guessed that they were in a form of stables. He turned and saw Billy, still blindfolded, being led towards him by the other man.

22

'Tell your friend to stay still. I will not warn him again,' said the masked man sternly.

Frog watched as both the men led their spiders into separate stalls. He could also see that the spiders wore a type of harness and reins, which the men now removed.

'Can you see what's happening?' asked Billy, tilting his head back and trying to see under his blindfold.

'Yes, we're in a big underground cavern where they keep the spiders and they're putting them into what look like stables. The whole place is lit up by weird crystals'

'How come you can see so much?' asked Billy.

'They've taken my blindfold off.'

'Why haven't they taken mine off?'

'I don't know,' said Frog. 'Perhaps we'll find out in a minute.'

'Can you get your hands free?' asked Billy as he twisted and turned his wrists behind his back.

'No, and I'm not sure what I'd do if I could.'

'Escaping would be a good idea.'

'At the moment, I don't know where we would run,' said Frog. 'We might end up in worse danger.'

'If it's a choice between being fed to giant spiders or running away,' said Billy as he continued to try to free his wrists, 'then I vote for running away.'

'Shush!' said Frog. 'Keep still. They're coming back.'

The two men stopped a short distance from the boys and had a quiet conversation. While they stood there, Frog noticed that both of them carried short, curved swords held at their waists, sheathed in highly decorated and ornate scabbards.

23

They turned their heads and stared in his direction. Frog felt both pairs of eyes studying him intently. He tried not to feel intimidated and firmly met their gaze. The men then turned back to each other and exchanged a few more words, until the man wearing the sand-coloured robes turned and walked back towards the rows of spiders in their stables.

'What's going on?' whispered Billy, shifting his hands again.

'Keep still. He's coming back,' warned Frog.

The man stood in front of Frog and stared down at him.

'You don't frighten me,' said Frog defiantly. 'It's easy to hide behind a mask; there's nothing brave about that,' he added.

The man reached up and pulled the cloth to one side to reveal a tanned face, which was surprisingly kind in appearance. He wore a short, dark moustache and tattooed on his right cheekbone was the image of a small, black spider.

'Be careful that you do not see too much for your own good,' he said.

'What are you going to do with us?' asked Frog.

'What is to be done with you has not yet been decided,' he replied. 'So you must now come with me.'

'I want my blindfold taken off,' said Billy.

'If you wish, but what you see may seal your fate,' said the man.

'I'll take my chances,' Billy boldly replied.

The man reached forwards and with one movement, released the blindfold.

Billy squinted at the light and looked at Frog.

24

'Hiya mate. Fancy seeing you here,' he grinned.

'It is well that you have a sense of humour,' smiled the man. 'We have a saying amongst my people. 'Better to laugh in the face of death than to cry for all eternity.'

'I'll try to remember that when I have my hands free,' said Billy, 'and I have something to fight with,' he added as an afterthought.

'Your bravery will be tested all in good time, but for now stop trying to free yourself. You only succeed in tightening your bonds by wriggling like a girl.'

This was too much for Billy and he launched himself head first at the man. What happened next took both Billy and Frog by surprise. The man swiftly stepped back and with one effortless movement swung Billy up and over his shoulder in a fireman's lift, with Billy's head facing forwards. A small, viciously serrated dagger appeared against Billy's throat.

'Do not struggle or, I promise you, there will only be scraps of you left to feed to my spider.' The tone of his voice was dark and chilling and it let both Billy and Frog understand that this was no idle threat. 'Now, be quiet, both of you. And you,' he motioned to Frog, 'walk ahead of me.'

They continued for some distance, down a long corridor, until they reached a solid stone wall, in front of which stood two, black-robed guards, their long scimitars held at the ready.

The two guards stepped aside and as they did so, the man carrying Billy reached out and caught Frog by the arm.

'Keep walking,' he commanded.

Whether he wanted to or not, Frog was propelled towards the granite wall.

This is going to hurt, he thought to himself as he shut his eyes and anticipated his face connecting with the rock. However, all he felt was a cool breeze passing over his face. He opened his eyes and the wall was now behind them; they had passed right through the solid rock!

'You're crazy. Let me down,' he heard Billy complain.

The man released Frog's arm and swung Billy down to his feet.

'What... What happened?' asked Billy.

'Magic,' replied Frog. 'But I'm wondering if it's good or bad,' he added.

They were standing in a cavern, which was bathed in the same bluish light from yet more crystal rocks placed on stone plinths, encircling a stone altar at the cavern's centre. An intense blue orb floated above the altar while four large statues looked down on the scene. Two of the figures had their faces obscured by stone hoods, whilst one of the others had the unmistakable features of his old friend Gizmo from Castellion. The final one next to it was of a beautiful, short-haired woman with high cheekbones and a lean, boyish face.

A hooded figure emerged from a shadowed recess and effortlessly floated towards them. It stopped within arm's length.

'Untie the small one's hands,' said a woman's soft voice.

The man obeyed without hesitation, releasing Frog, who rubbed his cramped wrists to bring the circulation back into them.

'Come with me,' the voice beckoned to Frog and he followed the figure to the altar.

'Do you see what the orb protects?' asked the woman.

Frog looked at the orb and could now discern the shape of the Rune Stone, floating inside it.

'Yes,' he replied. 'Is it a Rune Stone?'

'It is the Rune Stone of Aridian, of the Second Dimension and gateway to all other worlds and Dimensions. To prove to me that you are the Chosen One, you must reach into the orb and touch the Rune Stone's surface,' said the woman.

'Which Chosen One do you think I am?' asked Frog.

The woman ignored his question.

'The Rune Stone will decide if you are in the right place at the right time. If you are the Chosen One that we seek, then your brightness will be revealed to us all.'

'And what if it decides that I'm not the right one?' asked Frog.

'Then you will be consumed by its fire and left to burn for all eternity,' she replied.

'What if I don't want to take this test?' Frog asked.

Her voice took on a deeper, menacing tone. 'Then we will assume that you are an impostor and you and your companion will be fed to the Sandspiders.'

Frog weighed up his options and finally turned to face the hooded figure.

'For all I know, you could be an enemy of the Guardians and after the Rune Stone for your own use.'

'Let the Rune Stone decide,' she commanded.

Frog turned to face Billy. 'I'm sorry Billy, but if it's a choice of letting a Rune Stone fall into the wrong hands or being fed to giant spiders, we'll have to take our chances with the spiders. If you can remember Dollyo Chagi, then do it now.'

Billy stared at Frog for a second or two as he ran the Taekwondo move through his head and then he turned in one swift movement and brought his leg up and around to kick the surprised man in the ribs. The contact was perfect; the man doubled up and flew sideways gasping for breath.

'To me! To me!' shouted Frog as he unsheathed his sword and sidestepped the cloaked figure. He then ran towards one of the large statues and as Billy reached him, he turned him around and cut his bonds with the sword.

'Here, take this,' he told Billy handing him the sword.

'What are you going to use?' asked Billy.

'Oh, don't worry; I can be pretty handy with this,' replied Frog as he uncoiled his whip and let it loose with a loud crack.

The robed figure had turned to face them and the man was now recovering as he drew his curved sword and advanced on Billy and Frog.

'Sorry Billy,' said Frog. 'I didn't mean to get you into this.'

'That's okay,' shrugged Billy. 'Same as back home really. Your trouble is my trouble; your fight is my fight. That's what mates are for.'

Frog glanced up at the statue that towered over them.

'Gizmo, where are you when I need you?' he pleaded as the man raised his sword, its blade ready to scythe into the boy's heads.

3

Aridian

'Stop!' shouted the woman as her hands reached up and pulled back the hood of her cloak. Billy and Frog stared as the man's sword curved through the air with a swish and was brought down to one side and away from them in one effortless movement, the blade smoothly sliding back into its scabbard. For a moment, there was silence and Frog was not sure whether he and Billy should drop their guard or take advantage of the situation and run. Within seconds their minds were made up for them; the woman knelt before him and smiled into Frog's eyes.

'You are surely the Frog of legend,' she said. 'Your loyalty to the Guardians and to the safety of the Dimensions is unquestionable by your show of bravery. Your companion does you proud, although we had no knowledge that you would be accompanied. For all we knew you could have been instruments of Belzeera's making; she conspires to deceive us in many ways. She could have sent you to infiltrate our refuge and taint the sacred Rune Stone. That is why we have taken such cautious steps.'

She stood. 'I am Cassaria, Guardian of Aridian, and

this,' she gestured towards the man, 'is Ameer. He is Prince and leader of the Aridian people and the commander of its army.'

Frog and Billy stood, entranced by the woman's face. She had short, brown hair, which framed her lean, almost boyish features. A silver earring in the shape of a spider's web hung from one ear and two small black spiders were tattooed on each of her cheekbones. Even in the strange bluish light, she had the brownest eyes that either Billy or Frog had ever seen. In fact, they were so clear that Billy could see his own reflection in them.

Frog took his sword from the spellbound Billy and sheathed it.

'I am Frog of Castellion; although I wouldn't count myself as a legend,' he said as he coiled his whip. 'And this is my best friend, Billy Smart, whose journey here was totally unplanned.' He turned to Billy who was still lost in Cassaria's eyes.

'Billy!' said Frog elbowing him in the ribs.

'Sorry, what were you saying?' stammered Billy.

'I was introducing you and saying that this is your first visit to the Dimensions and as unexpected to me as it is for you,' said Frog.

'Well, I can't say that it isn't exciting,' said Billy.

Ameer stepped forward. 'You are brave and resourceful for one so young,' he said to Billy. 'You must show me that move of yours; I would not want to fall foul of it again,' he smiled, rubbing his side.

'Sure,' replied Billy. 'I have plenty of other ones where that came from.'

'I think that we had better find out what this is all

30

about and why we're here before you start showing off your Taekwondo,' said Frog.

Cassaria turned and indicated for them to follow. 'Come, you must be tired and thirsty from your journey. Let us retire to my chambers and Ameer and I can tell you all that you need to know.'

'Before we do,' said Frog, 'can you tell me about these statues. Is this a statue of you and is that one of Gizmo?'

'Yes and yes,' confirmed Cassaria.

He pointed around at the other two. 'Who are they and why can't we see their faces?'

'These images represent the Guardians of the Four Dimensions. The faces of those two will be revealed to you when the time comes for you to meet them and not before,' explained Cassaria.

'Surely, you can tell me how my friend Gizmo is?' pleaded Frog.

'I have not seen Gizmo for a very long time, but when we last communicated he was in good health, although he will have aged many years since you last met.

'But, I saw him only a few months ago,' said Frog.

'You seem to forget,' said Cassaria, 'that the passage of time between the Dimensions is affected by the Slipstream in different ways. It has indeed been many, many years since you were in Castellion.'

'What's happened to my friends?' asked Frog with concern.

'As far as I know they are all well, but older. Castellion is also safe, for the present,' said Cassaria. 'The threat now lies here on Aridian. Come, let us talk in more comfortable surroundings.'

They walked towards a wall which had a large spider carved in its centre.

'I'm not all that keen on melting through walls,' said Billy nervously.

'No matter,' said Cassaria as she reached forwards and pressed the centre of the symbol. The outline of a door appeared in the wall and it slid silently to one side allowing them to walk into a smaller chamber.

'Sit. Make yourselves comfortable while I prepare us some refreshment,' she told them as she disappeared into a side room.

Strewn out in front of them on a thick-carpeted floor was a circle of scattered cushions. At its centre sat a low wooden table with various parchment scrolls bundled to one side.

'Excuse me,' said Ameer. 'I will help my lady. Please, sit,' he gestured to them and followed Cassaria into the side room.

Frog and Billy turned to see that there was now a solid wall behind them and the same circular carving of a spider stared down at them.

'Neat,' said Billy as he pressed his hands against the unyielding stone. 'I bet she didn't learn that from Marvin's Magic.'

'Billy, you don't half whiff a bit,' said Frog.

'I've been thinking the same about you.'

'Perhaps it's that stuff that you trod in.'

'No,' said Billy. 'This is a sort of spidery smell.'

Frog leant forwards and sniffed at Billy's hair. 'Phew! It *is* you,' he said.

Billy grabbed Frog before he could move away and gave his head a quick sniff. 'You don't smell any better either, so stop going on about me,' he said.

'Well I don't think there's any chance of a shower around here so we're just going to have to live with it for now,' said Frog and looked around the room; it was decorated with colourful hanging rugs and a couple of stone plinths upon which sat crystal rocks that gave out the soft blue light. In a recess on the other side of the room was an Hourglass about 60 cm in height and Frog noticed that the sand was slowly trickling through it grain by grain, second by second and the contents were over two thirds through its cycle.

Billy had also spotted it and was making his way towards it.

'Leave it, Billy,' said Frog. 'If there's one thing that I've learnt it's not to touch anything until you're told that it's safe to do so. Come and sit down.'

Frog made himself comfortable on the cushions and noticed that one of the scrolls was partly rolled open. It looked like a map, but not like any map that he had seen before. There were grid lines across it, but that was where the similarity ended; everything else was circles and swirls. He was engrossed in trying to make sense of the patterns when suddenly there was a loud 'Zaaap!'

'Yeow!' shouted Billy.

Frog jumped to his senses as he looked up in Billy's direction.

Billy was standing near the Hourglass, his hair rigid and on end. Wisps of smoke floated up from his head and from his fingertips. His face was as white as a sheet.

'Billy, are you all right?' asked Frog.

Billy didn't answer; he was frozen to the spot and couldn't move.

Cassaria and Ameer suddenly appeared from the side room.

'What's happened to him?' asked Frog.

'I see that your friend Billy has an inquisitive nature. He will either learn quickly or he will pay for his curiosity,' she smiled as she walked towards him.

'The Hourglass is protected from prying hands by a Judgement Spell. He is lucky that it is designed only to capture and not to kill,' she continued. She then reached out her arms and brought the bangles together, which gave off a soft glow, and gently touched the sides of Billy's head with her fingers.

Billy blinked once, looked down at his smoking fingers, then up at Cassaria and fainted.

'Looks like you're going to learn the hard way, my friend,' said Frog. 'Just like me.'

Cassaria and Ameer gently carried Billy to the cushions.

'I'll get some salve for his hands,' said Cassaria, 'It will heal the burning quickly, although he will have to live with his singed hair for a while.'

Frog watched over Billy for the next few minutes as Cassaria and Ameer tended to his hands. Cassaria gently rubbed a green-looking paste into his now-very-red fingers, whilst Ameer dabbed at his hair with a damp cloth.

A tear slowly rolled from one of Billy's eyes and perched on his cheek.

'Don't touch it,' instructed Cassaria. She produced a

small glass tube from her robe and removed the stopper.

'With the right Magic, this can be used to help protect the boy,' and she allowed the tear to run into the tube and safely sealed it again, replacing it back within her robe.

Eventually, Billy opened his eyes and Ameer helped him to take a drink of a reviving potion that Cassaria had prepared.

'What bit of "Leave it, Billy" didn't you understand?' asked Frog.

'What's that burning smell?'

'You,' said Frog. 'And you're lucky that you weren't barbecued,' he added.

Billy looked down at his hands. 'They tingle.'

'They will for a while and then the redness will disappear,' said Cassaria. 'But I'm afraid you will have to wait for the scorch marks to grow out of your hair.'

Billy tried to get up but Cassaria stopped him. 'Rest,' she said, 'while we bring in the supper. You will feel much better when you have had something to eat.'

When Cassaria and Ameer had left the room, Frog hissed at Billy. 'You wazzuck! You'll get yourself killed. What did I tell you?'

'Sorry,' said Billy sheepishly.

'Listen to me in future, or I'll let them feed you to the spiders,' added Frog.

Cassaria and Ameer returned with wooden bowls and plates laden with bread and food. Frog moved the scrolls to the floor to make room for everything as Ameer returned with a large jug and some goblets.

'Eat, eat,' he encouraged as he and Cassaria passed around the plates.

Frog and Billy helped themselves to what appeared to be cooked vegetables, brown bread and strips of white chicken meat. It was some minutes before Ameer spoke again.

'How are you feeling now?' he asked Billy.

'Much better, thank you,' he replied helping himself to his sixth piece of meat. 'This chicken really is delicious.'

Ameer looked quizzically at Billy and then at Frog.

'Chicken,' repeated Frog picking a portion up for himself. 'You probably have another name for it here,' he added.

'Yes, you know, it's a bird with lots of feathers and flaps about but can't fly,' said Billy as he reached for yet another piece.

'We have birds on Aridian,' said Ameer. 'Most of them are carrion and taste rank and unclean. We do not eat them.'

'This is Serpens,' said Cassaria. 'In your world, I think that you call it snake.'

Billy froze for the second time that night and then he slowly placed the piece of meat back onto his plate. 'I think that I've had enough, thank you,' he said as he reached for his drink.

'It tastes like chicken,' said Frog still chewing on a piece.

'This is rock Serpens,' said Ameer. 'It's very hard to catch but well worth the effort as it is the most tender of meat. If you are out in the wastelands and cannot light a fire, you can eat it raw if need be.'

'No offence, but I'll stick to fruit from now on,' said Billy and picked up a round, green object from a dish. 'This is a fruit, isn't it?' he asked.

'Yes,' said Ameer. 'It is called Atemoya. We grow them in our plantation houses and they are very sweet. Here, let me,' he said, cutting it in half with a knife.

'You need to scoop out the flesh; use your fingers.'

Billy took a small amount between his fingers and tentatively put it into his mouth. 'Wow! It tastes wonderful,' he said wiping the juice from his chin. 'It's got a sort of custardy taste,' he explained to Frog before digging his fingers into the fruit again.

'You need to spit out the seeds,' said Ameer.

'Don't they taste very nice?' asked Billy.

'No,' said Ameer. 'And they are poisonous.'

Billy decided that he no longer wanted any more of the fruit, despite Ameer assuring him that as long as he didn't swallow too many of the seeds he would be all right. Billy also passed on the dried lizard's tongues and crystallised sand beetles, choosing to quietly sip his drink instead.

When they had all finished eating and Cassaria and Ameer had cleared away the dishes, they all sat around the low table, drinking a refreshing green tea, which, to Billy's relief, had no hidden ingredients or dangers.

'How much does Billy know of the Dimensions and your previous visit to Castellion?' Cassaria asked Frog.

'He has a rough idea of what happened on Castellion, but like me he does not know why he is here and what is happening,' replied Frog.

'Let me start with Aridian,' said Cassaria.

'For many generations, the good people of Aridian have existed and lived beneath the dry, scorched landscape, for it is here, below the world's surface, that the liquid of life is found – water.

'This is a world within a world, underground. The people live away from the desolate and hostile desert; their dwellings and communities are hewn into the bedrock of Aridian. Enormous caverns, vast enough to contain great lakes and watercourses, honeycomb throughout the sub-surface. Hot springs rise and give off steam as part of an underground ecosystem, which creates its own atmosphere where clouds of condensation gather and fall as rain.

'These organic, crystallised rocks grow on Aridian's surface.' She indicated to several of them around the room. 'They are fed by the twin sun's rays and, in turn, collect and store its power. The rocks generate heat and light according to their size, but the lifespan of even the largest is only about three months at the most. Then the rocks become a soft, brittle material that crumbles into coarse sand.

The crystal formations are protected and carefully maintained by the Aridian people, who regularly harvest them and transport them below ground to provide light and heat. Without the rocks, we would have to live a life governed by flame and firelight. Eventually smoke would choke and pollute our subterranean atmosphere and poison our water sources, leaving us to either perish in cold darkness or face the furnace of Aridian's surface.

'Our diet consists of a variety of root vegetables and fruit that grow on vines in the large underground gardens; these are fed by the mineral-rich water and are constantly bathed in the light from rock crystals. Apart from smaller catches like Serpens, our fresh meat supply comes mainly from the herds of large lizard-like animals called Saurs that are resident to Aridian. They are the largest predator of this world, feeding mainly on the smaller reptiles, other snakes, insects and spiders. We keep some stock underground and when that gets low we send out hunting parties to replenish it. Our clothes and material comes from spider silk, which is produced at Pelmore, one of our underground communities.' She paused to take a drink.

'In the history of the Dimension that is Aridian, this world once had water on its surface along with an abundant green landscape. Its people lived in peace and prosperity. Then, the distant sun, which gave us warmth and light, suddenly underwent a meta-morphosis, splitting itself into two twin orbs. Their heat intensified over a period of time and scorched and parched Aridian's surface, dried up the rivers and lakes and burnt away the atmosphere. Thousands of the population died before the alternative safe havens below the surface were developed and inhabited.

'Not all Aridians felt that this was the right existence and some saw no future living in the deep underground labyrinths. Very soon, a fraction was formed and they decided to try to build their new lives on the world above ground, craving the harsh, unnatural sunlight. They broke away from the underground community and sought shelter in the surface caves and crags of the scattered rock formations. These people became known as the Dreden. Over many decades, they adapted to the environment of Aridian's surface, but there was a price to pay.

'Generations of living in the desert climate and adapting to a harsh diet changed them into a resentful and aggressive people who became enemies with their former kinfolk. Their skin grew tanned and leathery, as they developed a high tolerance to the extreme temperatures and an ability to endure long periods without the need to drink. However, there always comes a time when water is critical for survival and this is when they attack us both above and below ground to raid our water sources and food stores.

'There has never been what could be called a war between us, just a continuing series of hostilities. When they are not fighting us, they argue and fight with each other. They live in scattered groups across Aridian's surface; it is only when a group of them becomes truly desperate that they attack us. Many times, we have tried to reason with them but they have had no overall leader, no one who would take responsibility to join them together so that we can encourage them to live in peace and harmony with us again.'

A deep shudder suddenly passed through the floor bringing dust clouds from the walls and ceiling. She stopped for a moment, listening, and then she was on her feet.

'The Rune Stone! She tries for the Rune Stone again,' Cassaria shouted as she ran towards the wall and pressed the stone carving. Ameer was also on his feet and he was heading for the doorway after Cassaria.

'Come on, Billy,' said Frog. 'We don't want to miss anything.'

As they re-entered the great cavern, Cassaria was standing before the altar, her arms raised up in front of the now-pulsing orb. The bangles on her wrists were glowing white-hot and she was chanting in a strange language. The ground shook again and then a low drone resonated around the cavern, gradually rising in pitch until it was shrill and unbearable.

Frog and Billy covered their ears as it vibrated around their heads and then penetrated their minds, numbing their thoughts. They sunk to their knees in pain and through half-closed eyes Frog saw that even Ameer was helpless, crouched against the far wall, his arms wrapped over his head.

A shrill, harsh voice resonated from the Rune Stone.

'The Stone shall come to me. I shall rise up and conquer the Dimensions. The Hourglass will be mine and then time shall be my slave. My brother's powers have been passed to me through the Slipstream and the Stone's energy feeds my strength. Resistance is useless. Give up the Stone. Now!'

The noise reached a shattering high pitch and pieces of the cavern's ceiling crashed down around them as the floor shook again. Cassaria was now suspended in mid-air, level with the floating blue orb. At once, she became enveloped in a white radiance, her arms outstretched and reaching into the orb. Frog could see that a gigantic battle of wills was being fought as Cassaria's figure wavered and rippled as if she had been turned into a thin veil of material. Another shudder and a statue toppled over and crashed forwards, the figure exploding into chunks of stone as it hit the floor.

41

Frog felt Billy's arm nudge him as another large chunk of rock smashed into the ground close by. He could see that Billy was trying to say something but his words were drowned out by the deafening noise.

'What is it?' Frog shouted back, not even hearing his own voice.

Billy mouthed another word and nodded his head towards Frog's belt. Frog looked down to see that his leather pouch was glowing with the same burning white light that surrounded Cassaria. His hand went inside and his fingers found the glass whistle. He brought it out of the pouch and it shimmered and sparkled brightly. As he stared at its brightness, Lady Dawnstar's voice cut through the deafening chaos and her image appeared in his mind.

'Another world and it has another use, my dear Frog. Blow it. Blow it with all your might.'

Frog brought the whistle to his lips. He took in as much breath as he could and pushed the air from his lungs so hard that it hurt. No sound came from the whistle but as he exhaled, it flew from his fingers and landed on the stone floor in front of him. It began to spin, turning faster and faster until it became a blur, then, without warning, it exploded, shattering into fragments of diamond white light, which melted into the walls of the chamber. Everything stopped: the sound, the vibrations and the destruction. Frog could now hear the beating of his heart and the pounding of blood in his ears. Dust settled around them and he saw the form of Cassaria in a heap on the floor, as the Rune Stone once again floated gently and peacefully in its blue orb above the altar.

4

The Gathering Fury

Belzeera shrieked with frustration and anger as splinters of light flew out of the glowing water that filled a stone dish in front of her. The shock knocked her twisted wand from her hand and it clattered across the floor.

'What Magic is this? The Guardian resists, but I sense the presence of another force.'

She kicked out at the white bones that lay strewn around on the floor of the cave then stretched out her hand and the wand floated back to her grasp. Her eyes turned black and her voice changed from a woman's shrill cry to a deeper, menacing tone. Lord Maelstrom's voice spoke though her and echoed around the cave.

'The Rune Child is here; the one they call Frog has come to Aridian. Very well, sister, our victory shall be all the sweeter when we spill his blood on the Rune Stone and the Slipstream becomes ours to control. All shall feel my wrath; I will inflict such pain on them that their screams shall be heard across all of the Dimensions. Make preparations, my sister; we shall cause such desolation on Aridian that it will forever stand as a testament to our power. Not one living thing shall escape. Its destiny is to be our servant and to become an instrument of our dark and terrible army. The Rune Stone and the Hourglass shall be ours and with their power I shall be reborn.'

Belzeera's eyes folded back into her head and she collapsed in a faint. A wicked and cruel grin remained on her face.

On the sand dunes below, a Dreden hunting party had seen the flash of light coming from the cave and slowly and silently made their way up the rocky slope. They were dressed in camouflage material that even Billy would have admired; it was made from reptile skin, which seemed to change colour, almost chameleon-like, as light and shadow passed across it. They stood at the entrance to the cave and prepared to attack, their jagged swords and spears at the ready.

The first of them slipped as soundless as a shadow into the cave and the three other shapes followed in rapid succession. Their eyes, already acclimatised to the dark, quickly picked out the cloaked figure that lay on the floor.

'Get up,' ordered one of the men, but there was no movement.

'Get up or I will run you through with my spear,' he shouted.

Still there was no movement. He cautiously moved forwards and jabbed the blade of the spear towards the figure, but a hand shot out from the robe and grabbed the spear's staff. Green static was sent crackling along its length until it reached the hand of its owner who froze in shock. The three other men raised their weapons and moved in to strike at the huddled shape, which suddenly rose up with a terrible screech and brought out a wand. The air crackled around the cave as jagged veins of electric green leapt from one man to another, rendering them motionless and powerless.

'So, what have we here?' jibed Belzeera as she folded back her hood to reveal herself. 'Four foolish Dreden if I am not mistaken.'

The men stared helplessly back at her in the flickering light.

'Speak up!' she commanded. 'Before I incinerate you where you stand.'

'Yes, we are Dreden,' said a tall, lean man. 'My name is Zebran and when I am free I will make you pay for this.'

'Brave words from one whose life could end with a mere wave of my wand,' said Belzeera. 'Are your friends as brave as *you* claim to be?'

'Let us loose and you will soon taste our anger,' said another of them as they all struggled to free themselves.

Belzeera sent out another shockwave of green static towards them and they all grimaced in pain and ceased their struggling.

'Who are you and what do you want with us?' asked Zebran through clenched teeth.

Plans quickly formed in Belzeera's mind. These four Dreden would be the first instruments that she would use to spread her evil Magic across Aridian.

'I am Belzeera and I possess Magic and powers that you have never seen before. I can give you back Aridian. I can show you how to reclaim what is rightly yours above and below ground, once and for all.'

45

'Why would you do that for us?' asked Zebran suspiciously.

'In return for your world, all I ask is to take back that which is mine: the Rune Stone and the Hourglass of Aridian.' Her eyes gleamed with fury.

'If I remember rightly,' said Zebran. 'The Rune Stone and the Hourglass are protected by the Guardian Cassaria and as legend has it, should not leave her protection for fear of their power destroying us all.'

Belzeera began to weave her spell, pulling a veil over the Dreden's minds and feeding on their inbuilt bitterness and mistrust.

'She is an impostor! I am the true Guardian and I have returned from exile to reclaim the Rune Stone and the Hourglass in order to restore balance. Many years ago, dark forces placed Cassaria here and I was cast out. She commands Aridian for her own desire. That is why you have never been allowed to take your true place as rulers of Aridian. Let me free you and your people. There will be no more raiding for food and water, no more fighting with each other. I can unite you against your true enemy and give you victory. Aridian will be yours!' she stared at them in triumph, watching her poisonous Magic infect their minds. She then released her hold on them, knowing that she now controlled their actions and deeds.

'What is it that you wish us to do?' asked Zebran as he and the others knelt before her.

'Follow me,' she commanded sweeping past them and out into the cold desert air.

She led them down the slope and out to a small clump of rocks which sat amongst the sandy expanse.

She reached inside a gap in the rocks and after a few moments withdrew her hand. Hanging by their venomous tails, she held four small black scorpions.

'Let me show you the power,' she said as she scattered the creatures before her onto the sand, raised her twisted wand and spoke in the wicked tongue of forbidden Magic. The green static reached out and spread across the tiny creatures, which glowed a pale fluorescent. Zebran and his group stepped back as the insects began to grow. The sound of their limbs and scaly bodies cracked as they stretched and enlarged until they were towering over the group, 3 metres or more in height. They snapped their vicious pincers as dark green venom dripped from the giant hooks on the ends of their tails.

'They are yours to command. Beasts of war to do your bidding,' said Belzeera in triumph. 'There will be many more at your disposal before the night is done. Now, climb onto their backs and ride; ride out to your scattered peoples and rally them to the cause.'

'What if they will not come? What if they will not listen to us?' asked one of the men.

'They will listen,' she said menacingly. 'They will hear my bidding through your voices and none will dare to disobey. They will come here, to me. I will create a citadel from these rocks,' she said pointing behind her. 'This is where your army will be forged and armed; this is where your destiny awaits. Vengeance and victory will be your reward.'

Cautiously at first, Zebran and his men mounted the giant scorpions, but once they were seated on their backs, they became more confident as they sensed their power over the creatures.

'North, south, east and west,' Belzeera commanded. 'Do my bidding.'

The four scorpions raised their pincers into the air and let loose piercing screams that echoed out into the desert night. They then scuttled away with uncanny speed and disappeared into the landscape.

Belzeera smiled, her white teeth flashing in the moonlight.

'Soon you will be free, dear brother and our powers will join as one. Aridian will fall and so shall the Dimensions as each Rune Stone is gathered. One by one, the Guardians will lose their ancient Magic. Their strength will fail and I will keep them captive in the Void so that they shall witness your return. Then they will be brought to tremble before you.'

She drew in a deep breath and set to work luring the living things of the desert into her service. She then cast the foundations of her fortress from the pale stone crags that jutted out of the sand as the menace of Lord Maelstrom stirred restlessly in his fragile prison.

The scorpion that carried Zebran out across the desert finally brought him to a Dreden settlement and he slowed the creature as he approached, aware that the perimeter guards would have already alerted others to his presence. Twenty or so figures rose up out of the sand around him, spreading out in a circle and keeping well back from the menacing beast, their weapons ready to attack.

'Hold steady,' he shouted. 'My name is Zebran and I

am of the southern Dreden. I ask for council with your leader.'

'How would a Dreden acquire such a creature let alone master the ability to control it?' asked one of the figures.

'That is for me to discuss with your leader. Now, either grant me council or I will truly demonstrate how much control I have over it,' he replied. To emphasise the matter, he tapped the back of the scorpion's head and it raised its pincers, snapping them loudly above the men's heads.

The group receded a little as an individual figure broke away to quickly disappear into a cave between the large crags of stone. An uneasy silence followed and after a short while, more armed people spilled out from the cave until as many as three hundred of them surrounded Zebran and his mount. He noticed that despite any fear of the scorpion, they would not hesitate to attack him or the creature if the command was given.

'Zebran of the southern Dreden, I give you council,' shouted a voice. 'Come down and speak face to face. You are given safe passage as long as your creature behaves itself.'

Zebran slid down from the scorpion and walked towards the man who now stood forward from the group. He was over 6-foot tall, his lean face framed by long strands of lank blond hair, and he was dressed in the lizard skin clothes of the Dreden. Dawn was coming and the light made the leathery skin on his arms and face look a deathly pale.

'The heat will be with us soon and we will need to

take our rest. Whatever you have to say had better be quick and of value,' he said.

Zebran opened his mouth and the words of Belzeera poured from his tongue, influencing all who heard them, filling their minds with her promises of victory and the spoils of war. Eventually, there was not a man, woman or child who were not convinced to follow him and join the gathering fury that would form the great army whose sole intent would be to claim Aridian for themselves. Most were ready to destroy all who stood in their way, but there were also those who were wary and felt that the fight should be honourable and without needless bloodshed.

Over the coming weeks, as events unfolded on other parts of Aridian for Frog and Billy, Belzeera's messengers spread her words with a poisonous, hypnotic effect, gathering Dreden from all over Aridian's surface until they made their way to where she had used her vile Magic to create a black granite stronghold. Looking like a gigantic termite mound, rising up a thousand metres, its pinnacles reached up out of the sand and into a dark, menacing cloud.

She welcomed them all with wicked glee, putting them to work to construct weapons and war machines from the unnatural elements that she had conjured up. She had not only created an army of giant black scorpions for use as the Dreden's cavalry, but she had also used her wicked Magic to transform four harmless desert geckos into enormous, ugly, grey lizards. These were now her personal bodyguards and captains, and there were always at least two by her side, blood-red tongues constantly flicking in and out of their reptilian mouths, their narrow eyes ever watching with suspicion. They were her watchers, her spies. In fact, she had sent two of them out across the land to burrow into the underground passages, to spy and bring back news of what plans the Aridians were making to defend themselves. Nothing would stand in her way to ensure that the Rune Stone and the Hourglass would fall into her hands and, in the process, she would release her brother from the Void and make the conquest of the Dimensions a reality.

5

Let the Light …

Ameer was quickly on his feet and the first to reach the huddled shape that was Cassaria. Frog and Billy saw him catch his breath as he turned her body over and pulled back her robe.

'Is she …?' Frog could not bring himself to say the word.

'She still breathes,' answered Ameer as he gently lifted her body and carried her over the rubble and back into her apartments. Frog and Billy followed in concerned silence as Ameer laid her down on the cushions and it was then that the boys saw what had caused him to gasp. Her hair was now entirely a blue-white colour, even her eyebrows and her eyelashes. Her skin was colourless.

'What's happened to her?' asked Billy.

'I'm not sure,' said Ameer. 'But I think that the Rune Stone has drained her life force. She seems all but dead to us.'

He bowed his head and Frog could see that his face was creased with pain and sadness.

'I vowed to protect her from all harm and I have failed her,' he said.

Frog knelt beside Ameer and reached out to take Cassaria's hand in his. He noticed that there was a ring bearing a familiar emblem on one of her fingers. It had the intricate pattern of a crown etched in the centre of a burning sun. As he looked deep into the fiery design, a warm orange glow began to fill the room.

Ameer looked up and stared at Frog, whose face was bathed in a soft radiance.

'I don't want to freak you out,' said Billy. 'But your forehead is on fire!'

The familiar light of Castellion's Chosen radiated from Frog's brow and seemed to channel itself into Cassaria's body; the ring glowed and mirrored the image on Frog's forehead. Slowly, Cassaria opened her eyes and on seeing Frog, a smile formed on her lips.

'Let the Light free us from evil,' she said softly.

'Let the Light free us from evil,' whispered Frog.

For a while, they all sat in silence, bathed in the golden light, which passed between Frog and Cassaria. Slowly, it began to fade and they could see that Cassaria had regained a healthy pallor. Her hair, however, remained a striking bluish white with darker veins of blue running through the strands. Her eyes were also tinted with the same colours. She sat up and Ameer poured a goblet of water for her, which she took gratefully and sipped slowly.

'How do you feel?' he asked, still with concern on his face.

'I feel cleansed and refreshed, which I'm sure I have our friend Frog to thank for,' she said. 'For a moment I thought that I had lost the battle. That witch was in my mind; she was devouring my spirit and taking strength from the Rune Stone itself. There was also another darker, deeper presence helping her, adding strength to her powers. I fear that Lord Maelstrom is using her as an instrument to bring him back from the Void. They challenge the ancient Magic of the Guardians and plan a terrible destiny for Aridian and the Dimensions.'

'Who is this witch?' asked Billy.

'Belzeera, sister of the most evil Lord Maelstrom,' she answered.

'I didn't know that she was his sister,' said Frog.

'She has the same wicked streak in her and shares her brother's desires to conquer and dominate all,' said Ameer.

'It would seem that her brooding vengeance has been the catalyst to free her from what has kept her ensnared for so long in the Void,' said Cassaria.

'Is the Rune Stone safe now?' asked Frog.

'Balance has been restored and it is protected once more by the high Magic. However, I must consult the other Guardians for guidance as I sense that the Rune Stone has made some connection with me that I am yet to understand,' said Cassaria.

'I think that you need to see how the Rune Stone has affected your appearance,' said Ameer and he rose and rushed to the side room.

'Can you remember what happened?' asked Frog.

Cassaria furrowed her brow. 'I recall the orb drawing me in and my hands embracing the Rune Stone. Belzeera was trying to pull it from my grasp. I heard her vile Magic in my mind, telling me to release the Rune Stone, to give in. She filled my thoughts with sorrow and misery; hopelessness was suffocating me. It was as though I was drowning in despair. Then there came a sound, like a high-pitched note vibrating though the air. A soft breeze ran through me, scattering her wicked spell and I heard her scream with surprise and rage as streaks of blue light exploded through my senses. The next thing I remember is a soft golden glow filtering through my eyelids and opening them to see you.'

Ameer returned and handed Cassaria a small oval mirror and she spent a few moments studying herself.

'It's a shame that you broke your glass whistle,' said Billy.

'It's a good job that you pointed it out to me,' said Frog.

'Glass whistle?' asked Cassaria.

Frog then told her of what had happened to the rest of them while she was fighting to keep the Rune Stone safe from Belzeera.

'It never ceases to amaze me how the powers of the Dimensions link together in times of adversity,' she said. 'Who would have thought that an instrument from the Bird Men of Castellion would come into play after all these years to fight against the dark forces here on Aridian?'

'How did Lady Dawnstar know that we were in trouble?' asked Billy.

'She and Frog are joined through the powers of the Chosen: a sort of telepathy,' explained Cassaria.

'Why can't I sense her now?' asked Frog.

'The mystery of the Slipstream decides when connections between the Dimensions are made,' said Cassaria.

'Just let me try,' said Frog, closing his eyes.

They all watched in silence at the immense concentration on his face until, after a few minutes, he opened his eyes again.

'Nothing! I've tried to link with them all – Lady Dawnstar, Gizmo, Ginger, Fixer and Logan, even Sir Peacealot – but it's like an empty space,' he said with disappointment.

'If the need arrives I'm sure that a way will be found,' said Cassaria. 'Meanwhile, there is work to be done. We must find out what Belzeera is up to. I fear that there is more mischief on the surface than we have seen for many an age.'

'I am sure that it will soon be dawn-rise,' said Ameer. 'I will alert my commanders and send out reinforcements to the crystal farms. I think that it would also be wise to dispatch some scouting parties to see what the Dreden are up to. I for one do not like surprises. The time of rest will soon be upon us and we must replenish our strength. I will find quarters for Frog and Billy so that they can take their sleep. When we rise, I will introduce them to our lifestyle and customs so that they can become familiar with their new surroundings.'

'Sleep?' exclaimed Billy. 'How can I sleep with all this excitement?'

'Have you any idea what the time is?' asked Frog.

'Not a clue.'

'Look,' said Frog holding up his wrist and showing Billy his watch. It still read 17.45. 'That's the time back home.'

'Yeah. Neat, isn't it? And your point is?'

'How long do you think that we've been here?' asked Frog.

'How do I know, you're the one with the watch,' said Billy.

'By my reckoning, about ten hours. This means that we're going to get a really bad case of jet lag if we don't get some sleep and believe me, once you put your head on a pillow you'll be out for the count.'

'You sound just like my Mum.'

'Frog is right, Billy,' said Cassaria. 'The effect of the Slipstream will cloud your mind and if you do not get some rest you will not be at your best.'

'Besides,' added Ameer, 'if you are going to ride with us tomorrow night, I want you wide awake and alert.'

'Ride on those spiders again?' asked Billy.

'As I said, you will need to know as much as you can about Aridian and this time you will not be wearing a blindfold,' said Ameer.

'Now I really won't be able to sleep!' said Billy.

They walked back to the main chamber and stepped over the broken rocks that lay in the doorway.

'What a mess,' remarked Frog.

'The Rune Stone will repair the damage,' said Cassaria. 'Look, it has already begun.'

Billy and Frog watched in wonder as large chunks of rock lifted themselves up and floated back into the cracks and holes of the damaged walls and ceiling. Fragments of the statue and its column reassembled and righted themselves. The damage was being repaired around them in slow motion. As Cassaria guided them across the cavern, fragments of stone rose up, and then sought out their original place to fit seamlessly back into position.

'We will meet again before your next journey, but now I must consult my fellow Guardians,' said Cassaria, turning to the Rune Stone and the altar.

As they stood facing the entrance wall, Ameer put his hands on Frog and Billy's shoulders.

'Just walk forwards with me,' he said. 'Close your eyes if you don't want to look.'

Again, they had no choice. As Ameer stepped forwards, he gently put his weight behind them so that they were pushed through the stone.

'I just don't think that I could ever get used to that,' said Billy as he stood outside in the corridor looking back at the wall.

'Believe me, Billy, you will have to encounter stranger things,' said Ameer. 'Now follow me. We must get you some comfortable quarters so that you may rest.'

They followed Ameer along the corridors until they smelt a familiar odour and, turning a corner, they found themselves back to where the giant spiders were housed in their stables.

'For now, you can bed down in my quarters. There is plenty of room,' said Ameer leading them along the rows of open-fronted pens. As they passed by, Billy and Frog could see the dark, bulky bodies of sleeping spiders and they noticed that a strange emblem hung over every pen. Each one was different in design and colour.

They reminded Frog of Egyptian hieroglyphics.

'What do the signs mean?' he asked.

Ameer stopped them by a particularly large shape, its body rising and falling rhythmically with the breath of sleep, and pointed to the centre of the design.

'This is the spider's name. The other symbols around it signify its place and date of birth and the name of its rider and companion.'

'Yes, but what does it mean in plain language?' asked Billy.

'This spider was born on the second full moon, one hundred and twenty years ago in the main hatcheries at Pelmore, a city only a few miles from here. Its present rider and companion is Sanwar and the spider's name is Arac-Hun,' explained Ameer.

'Wow,' said Billy. 'A hundred and twenty? That's really old.'

'Not for an Aridian Sandspider,' said Ameer. 'They can grow to be over two hundred years of age.'

'Who gives them their names and who chooses their riders?' asked Frog.

'There is much for you to learn, but now is not the time,' replied Ameer leading them to a hallway that branched off from the stables. 'Hopefully I will be able to take you to Arachnae soon, which is the training ground for the spiders and their riders, but for now we must rest.'

He pulled back a curtain to reveal a canopied room.

'My house is your house,' he said bowing.

The boys stepped inside what felt like a large tent. The décor and furnishings were Arabic in style and design. A soft light filled the area and Frog noticed several small crystals seated in a wooden chandelier suspended from the centre of the room. Ameer led them to a curtained area, which contained cushions and bedding.

'If you are thirsty, there is water in the jug over there,' he said. 'Now you must sleep and refresh your senses. Should you need me I will not be far away. I will come and wake you at evening rise.' He let the curtain fall back into place and they saw his shadow recede into the room.

Frog unbuckled his belt and sword and pulled off his tunic, placing them all in a pile beside him, then he lay down among the soft pillows.

'Come on, Billy, let's get some sleep,' he said.

'I'm not really tired, but if there's nothing else to do I may as well keep you company,' said Billy as he sat down beside Frog. 'I can't wait to ride those spiders tomorrow, can you?'

'Billy, go to sleep,' said Frog.

'I told you; I'm not tired,' said Billy, propping himself up on a couple of pillows.

'You can't stay awake while everyone else sleeps,' said Frog. 'Now shut up and close your eyes.'

'I told you; I'm not sleepy,' yawned Billy as he sunk back into the pillows with his eyelids fluttering.

Frog watched as Billy's eyes closed and within a few seconds, the soft buzz of a snore escaped from the slumbering boy.

'Sweet dreams, Billy. Sweet dreams,' said Frog as he turned onto his side and allowed his own mind to drift into the gentle arms of sleep.

6

Arac – Khan

The sound of voices pulled Billy from a dreamless slumber and, for a moment, he wasn't sure where he was. The events of the previous night slowly came back to him as he rubbed the sleep from his eyes and took in his surroundings. There was no sign of Frog, but he could hear his friend's voice coming from somewhere behind the curtained screen.

'Well, this feels different already,' said Frog. 'It's surprisingly cool. I thought that I would be hot and uncomfortable.'

'It's designed to keep you cool in the heat of the sun and warm at night when the temperature drops,' said Ameer. 'If you need any help fitting it I will assist you when you're ready.'

Billy pulled back the drape and walked to the centre of the tented room. Ameer was sitting cross-legged at a low table, drinking from a small bowl.

'Awake at last, young Billy. So much sleep for one who was not tired,' he said smiling.

'What's the time?' asked Billy.

'It will soon be moonrise and time to go,' Ameer replied. 'You had best have some food before we leave

61

as we will not eat again until we reach Arachnae.' He indicated the table, which was laid out with various fruits and what looked like pancakes.

'Where's Frog?' enquired Billy as he sat down and picked up a small, brown, wrinkled fruit.

'Getting dressed,' answered Ameer.

'What's this?' asked Billy, inspecting the fruit closely.

'A fresh fig. You only eat the inside as the skin is quite tough.'

'We have these back home. My mum buys them from the health food shop, but I don't think that they're as fresh as this.'

'Here, let me show you,' said Ameer. He took another fig from the bowl and demonstrated how to open it and eat the pink contents. Billy followed suit and was pleasantly surprised with the taste. He then cast his eyes over the rest of the food.

'Is there anything else here that's not snake meat or poisonous?' he asked.

'Of course,' said Ameer with a chuckle. 'This is flat bread, these are dates and this is Atemoya mixed with sweet juice and don't worry, the seeds have been taken out.'

Billy ate hungrily, as Ameer rose and disappeared behind a screen. As he ate, he could hear the muffled voices of Frog and Ameer in conversation. After a short while, he was just about to pick up some more dates when Ameer came out from behind the screen followed by Frog. He was dressed in the sand-coloured robes of an Aridian.

'I'm getting worried about you,' said Billy. 'You're turning into a bit of a costume freak.'

'What's wrong with this?' asked Frog.

'It's a bit girly if you ask me.'

'I should get used to it if I was you.'

'No skin off my nose,' replied Billy.

'Good,' said Frog, smiling. 'Because there's one back there for you.'

'No way!' said Billy. 'You're not going to catch me wearing one of those.'

'If you want to survive while you are here on Aridian then you will need to wear our clothing,' said Ameer.

'I'll take my chances,' said Billy stubbornly. 'I can survive without making a bad fashion statement.'

Ameer got to his feet, took Billy gently by the arm and led him to the screen. Fifteen minutes later, Billy stood in front of Frog and Ameer. He was now wearing the traditional robes and headdress of the Aridian people.

'Excellent,' said Ameer. 'You look resplendent.'

'I feel like a wazuck!' replied Billy.

Ameer looked at Frog.

'He feels like a fool and an idiot,' Frog translated.

'You are wearing the attire of a proud Aridian tribesman. Please give it respect. It may well save your life,' said Ameer sternly. 'Now let us go; we must meet with the scouting parties.'

Ameer turned and strode out of the room with Frog and Billy quickly at his heels.

'This feels too weird,' said Billy. 'It's like wearing a dress.'

'How would you know? You haven't been trying on your sister's clothes have you?' teased Frog, laughing.

Billy turned a shade of red. 'Don't ever tell her about this,' he pleaded. 'She'll never let me live it down.'

'Don't worry, your secret's safe with me. Now try not to trip over. Just walk normally and you'll soon get used to it,' he encouraged.

By the time they had reached the far end of the stables, Frog was pleased to see that Billy was no longer waddling like a pregnant duck. It was just as well because there was quite a gathering of people waiting for them. Ameer guided Billy and Frog into the centre of the group, who were all wearing sand-coloured robes except one man who stood apart and was dressed in black and orange.

'On behalf of the Guardian Cassaria, I present to you Frog of the Chosen and his companion Billy,' Ameer announced.

As one, the group touched their foreheads and bowed.

'Step forward and return the gesture,' whispered Ameer.

Frog and Billy quickly did as they were told.

'They are to join our scouting parties this night and ride with us,' he continued.

It was then that the orange and black-robed man stepped forward. The whites of his eyes stood out from his deep brown face, and he wore a jet-black beard, which gave him a most fearsome appearance.

He spoke with suspicion. 'So, the rumours are true; you have accepted two young strangers into our midst and endangered our security because you believe them to be allies of the Guardians. We have been told what the witch is capable of. They could be creatures of her making.'

'They have satisfied Cassaria and also proved themselves in my eyes,' said Ameer.

'That may be, Lord Prince, but you know that they must endure the Sensing to be truly accepted and they cannot ride until they have been accepted.'

'Frog, Billy, this is Sand Master Katar. He is the stable master and custodian of the Sandspiders,' said Ameer. 'It is written in the ancient laws that he must be obeyed on any matters regarding the Sandspiders.' Ameer turned to Katar. 'They have already ridden and been scented,' he said. 'They were brought in from the desert by Alban and myself. The Sandspiders accepted them without hesitation.'

Katar leaned over Frog and Billy and vigorously sniffed at them.

'They have the scent, but they have not been accepted by Arac-Khan and as you know,' repeated Katar, 'they should not be allowed to ride until that initiation has been fulfilled.'

'Which is why now seems as good a time as any,' responded Ameer. 'We will ready the scouting parties while you conduct the Sensing.'

'You seem confident that they will pass the test,' said Katar.

'I have every confidence in these boys. Besides, as I have said, they have Cassaria's blessing,' said Ameer.

'No doubt,' said Katar. 'But let us see if they really deserve to wear these robes.'

He guided Frog and Billy away from the group and towards a narrow corridor between two of the pens.

'Where are we going?' asked Frog.

'To meet Arac-Khan,' replied Katar.

'Who's Arac-Khan when he's at home?' asked Billy.

'Have patience,' said Katar. 'Now, no more questions.'

Frog couldn't help noticing that Katar had a knowing grin on his face and a gleam was in his eyes.

As they continued down the corridor, the spider scent became stronger and as they breathed it in, Frog and Billy started to feel lightheaded, almost drugged. By the time that they stepped into a large, shadowy cave, their thoughts had taken on a dream-like quality and everything seemed to be happening in slow motion.

Katar guided them to the centre of the cave. It seemed empty except for sand and some straw-like material scattered around on the floor. Its recesses were lost in darkness. Katar stood in front of them, leaning forwards and looking into their eyes so that his face became distorted in their vision.

'Even a Guardian can be tricked,' he said, staring into Frog's eyes. 'Perhaps you are not the true Frog after all. I do declare that Arac-Khan will make short work of you both and expose you for what abominations you really are.'

He moved silently into the shadows leaving Frog and Billy standing alone, confused and dazed.

'Are you okay, Billy?' asked Frog.

'Something's not right. I feel strange,' said Billy. 'My head feels all fuzzy.'

'Me too,' said Frog. 'Be on your guard and stay close to me.' Before he could say anything else, a large, previously unnoticed figure in the corner of the room moved slowly towards them. Its shape and bulk emerged from the shadow to reveal the largest spider that they had seen so far. This one was enormous, towering over them by at least 4 metres. It stopped a short arm's length away and its fetid breath washed over them. Its giant mandibles slowly twitched and its six black eyes studied them intensely.

'I'd run, but for some reason I can't move,' said Billy.

'Neither can I,' replied Frog.

'I suppose we'd better be nice to it then,' added Billy.

Silence! said a harsh rasping voice in Billy's head. *Do you not know who I am?*

'I guess that you're Arac- Khan,' said Billy.

Which one of you claims to be the Chosen one called Frog? the spider's voice thundered in Frog's head.

'That would be me,' he answered.

Your human voices scratch my senses. Do not use your tongues; use your thoughts, commanded the spider.

'I don't particularly like you inside my head,' said Billy. 'But if you're trying to frighten us, you're not doing a very good job,' he added bravely.

'Billy, be quiet,' said Frog, but it was too late.

So you want to be frightened, do you? said the spider. *Well, let me oblige you.*

Suddenly, it lunged its front two legs forwards and grabbed Billy by the ankles, raising him high into the air so that he hung upside down. Then it began to swing him from side to side.

'Put me down,' yelled Billy. 'I hate heights. Put me down.'

'Put my friend down,' said Frog. 'If you harm him, so help me, when I get free I'll make you pay dearly.'

Brave words from one who is so helpless, hissed the spider in Frog's head. *How would you like to join your friend?*

'If it's a choice of him or me up there then let him down and take me,' said Frog.

Not only brave but loyal too, said the spider. *These are fine qualities. What say you, Arac-Khan?*

A gentle, female voice entered Frog and Billy's heads. *They are not the qualities of a witch's creation. Bring them to me so that I may complete the Sensing.*

The spider slowly lowered Billy, who had gone quite pale. It lifted him to his feet and guided him along with Frog to the rear of the cave. Slowly, a soft light began to illuminate their surroundings and they could see a small, orange-robed figure who was uncovering several of the light-giving crystals. As their eyes adjusted to the new level of light, they could also see another spider nestled among a straw bed. It was pure white in colour and no bigger than a metre in size.

Behold, the real Arac-Khan, said the giant spider. *If you make any aggressive moves towards her, I will squash you where you stand.*

'I don't feel very well,' moaned Billy, who now looked a rather green colour.

'You need to drink this,' said a girl's soft voice. Then the figure in the orange robe stepped forwards with a cup and offered it to Billy's lips. 'Drink it slowly. It will work quickly and clear your head then you will gradually be free to move.'

Frog studied the girl's features and guessed that she

was older than him by a couple of years. She had a fresh, freckled face; her dark eyes reflected the light from the crystals and her fair hair was tied in a short braid. She had the fine black image of a spider tattooed on her cheek.

Billy took a couple of mouthfuls of the thick, sweet liquid and felt it run down his throat. Its cool flow quickly spread through his body and cleared his mind.

'Thank you,' he said.

'My name is Nadiah,' she replied then took the cup to Frog and helped him to drink.

Arac-Khan spoke gently to Billy. *Come and sit by me.*

Billy did as he was asked and sat in the straw next to the white spider.

Starting to feel better? asked Arac-Khan.

'Yes thanks,' said Billy.

Good, but do try to talk with your thoughts. You will find it much easier, said Arac-Khan. *Now, I'm going to ask you some questions. Is that all right?*

'Sure,' replied Billy. 'Sorry,' he corrected himself and thought the words. *Ask away.*

Arac-Khan reached forward with her two front legs and placed them on either side of Billy's head. Billy grinned.

What is it? asked Arac-Khan.

It tickles, replied Billy.

Just relax, close your eyes and try to think of something nice.

Billy did as he was told and then there was a soft flash; it was as if the inside of his eyelids had lit up like a cinema screen. He could see himself sitting around a table with his parents and his sister. It was last

Christmas day and they were having their Christmas dinner. Everyone was smiling and laughing and Billy remembered the warm feeling that he had. His dad was in the army, serving abroad and had not been expected to be home until after the New Year, but three days before Christmas they received a phone call from him. He had been unexpectedly awarded leave and was going to be one of the lucky ones to be sent home in time for Christmas day.

When he walked through the door on Christmas Eve, nothing else mattered. It had been a perfect Christmas.

Billy smiled again at the memory then there was another flash and the image was gone. He opened his eyes to stare into the multi-eyed face of Arac-Khan.

You are a very human being, said Arac-Khan. *No evil could conjure up such good thoughts. I also sensed that you have many good values and qualities. It is nice to meet you, Billy Smart, son of James Smart the warrior. Two things I would ask of you. Firstly, be kinder to my smaller kinfolk who live in your world; you have nothing to fear from them. Secondly, have more patience with your little sister; she is learning and growing just like you and she loves you dearly.*

You learnt all that from me in those few seconds? asked Billy.

And so much more, said Arac–Khan. *Now, go to Nadiah and take some more to drink while I meet the one who is called Frog.*

Arac-Khan beckoned Frog to sit by her, which he also did.

Just open your thoughts to me, she said as she placed her front legs on Frog's head.

Frog thought of his home, his family and friends then, all at once, he found himself back in Castellion, his past adventures flashing across his mind. Billy and Nadiah watched as Frog's forehead took on a golden glow, which filled the cave. The gigantic spider shifted uneasily, but Nadiah looked in its direction and Billy sensed that something was said to reassure the spider that nothing was wrong. It wasn't long before the glow had spread and the intense golden light surrounded both Frog and Arac-Khan.

'I have never witnessed a Sensing such as this,' Nadiah whispered to Billy. 'Your friend must be very special.'

'He's full of surprises all right,' said Billy smiling.

Frog's life unfolded in a picture show; memories that he had forgotten pushed their way out from the recess of his mind and then skittered away into his subconscious in a brief moment. The seconds following his birth were revealed to him and then unrecalled thoughts of his younger years paraded past in the blink of an eye. Thirteen years of emotions and experiences merged into a carousel of images and then, abruptly, his mind went blank, leaving him dizzy and disorientated. Slowly, he opened his eyes and stared into the face of Arac-Khan.

If ever I saw a spider smile, it would be now, thought Frog.

The voice of Arac-Khan spoke in Frog's head. *Welcome Frog, born of the boy Christopher. You are a long way from home, but do not fear. The Sensing is*

*complete and there is no doubt that you are the Frog of
the Chosen. I also see that you are no stranger to the
meeting of minds; you have an affinity with the lizards
of the air. The Dragons of Castellion have endowed you
with their kinship.*

*Katar, these boys are genuine. Watch over them and
ensure that the colony embraces their presence.*

Katar approached from a recess in the cave and
turned to Billy and Frog.

'You must forgive me for my suspicions, but I serve
no one but Arac-Khan and I protect her with my life if
necessary. By her bidding I extend the same duty to
you both.' He touched his forehead and gave a low bow.
'You need to return to Prince Ameer in readiness for
your journey into the desert. I would join you but
unfortunately, I am needed in other places. Therefore,
Nadiah will be your companion and guide; she will
devote herself to your protection and safety.'

Katar bowed once more and then made his exit back
down the passageway.

Billy turned to Nadiah and said, 'I don't mean to be
rude, but firstly, you're a girl and secondly, I don't think
that you'll be much help in a fight. Frog and I will end
up protecting you!'

Nadiah positioned herself defiantly in front of Billy,
her hands hung innocently by her sides. 'I assure you
that I am capable of looking after myself and others for
that matter.'

'I doubt if you've come across someone who uses
Taekwondo. I'm a third Kup and I could easily deal with
you,' said Billy, getting slightly carried away with
himself.

Frog saw the gentle smile on Nadiah's face and the mischievous gleam in her eyes. She slipped her hands quickly in and out of the folds in her robes and they gave off a soft blue glow.

'Billy, I think that you should apologise and accept that Nadiah is capable of looking after herself.'

'All I'm saying is that we'll most likely be taking care of her,' said Billy.

'Then you won't have a problem when someone does this,' announced Nadiah and drew her hands forwards in a pulling motion in front of Billy's legs. He could do nothing as they scissored out from beneath him and gravity deposited him onto his backside. She hadn't even made contact with him.

Nadiah smiled down at him in satisfaction.

'How? How?' he stammered looking around him and then up at her in awe.

She offered her hand to him and Billy nodded, taking it with grace and getting to his feet.

'I apologise. Sometimes I've got a big mouth,' said Billy.

'Apology accepted,' said Nadiah. 'Now we must go; the others will be waiting.'

Before they moved off back down the passageway, Arac-Khan bade them a safe journey and passed a solitary message to Frog, which none of the others sensed. Frog nodded back to the spider in acknowledgement and understanding.

'That was a pretty neat move that you pulled on me back there,' Billy said to Nadiah. 'You'll have to teach me how to do it.'

'And you will have to instruct me in your

Taekwondo. I understand from Ameer that you are quite adept in the art,' she replied.

'You know about that?'

'I already know many things about you, Billy Smart. You have made an impression on me,' she replied.

'I guess that we're even then,' said Billy as he rubbed his aching bottom.

7

Skirmish

Billy, Frog and Nadiah had met up with Amcer and a dozen or so riders at a large entrance hall just a short walk from the stables. It was here that the riders had readied their mounts and the air was heavy with the musk of spiders. The great beasts were lined up on either side of the hall, their polished, dark leather and metal harnesses catching and reflecting the light of the crystals. Ameer then took Frog to meet with Cassaria once again. Now, while everyone else waited for them to return, Billy stood fidgeting with his robes.

'Are you all right?' asked Nadiah.

'I don't feel comfortable in these clothes,' replied Billy as he pulled at the material for the umpteenth time.

'Here, let me help you,' she said and before he could object, Nadiah had her arms around his waist, untying the belt and loosening the robes. 'What's this lump in the folds?' she asked.

'Just some food for later on in case I get hungry,' Billy quickly explained.

'It will only get warm in there. Let me take it out,' she said.

'No. No, it's all right. Just leave it where it is,' he said getting slightly agitated.

'All right, don't panic. I'm only trying to help.'

Billy stood there, his face reddening by the second, hoping that no one would notice and praying that Frog would not return at this moment to see his predicament.

'Just relax and trust me,' she instructed and tugged at the robe, at one point reaching underneath to adjust the undergarment. This caused Billy's eyes to widen in surprise and horror as a new level of embarrassment struck him. Finally, to his relief, she wrapped the belt around his middle and tied it in a half knot.

'How does that feel now?' she asked stepping back to inspect him.

'Much better,' said Billy. 'Sorry I snapped at you.'

'Don't worry, I don't get upset that easily,' she replied.

'Hey, it's surprisingly comfortable,' he added walking around in a small circle, testing his movements. 'If I didn't feel so stupid, I could get used to it.'

One of the riders heard and flashed a stern glance at him.

'No offence meant,' said Billy hastily.

At that moment, Ameer and Frog appeared, striding towards them from across the cavern. Both of their faces wore uneasy looks.

'Something troubles them,' observed Nadiah and Billy noticed that she gave a sudden shiver.

'Are you cold?' he asked.

'Not cold, just a feeling that something is not right, a feeling that we are being watched,' she replied as her eyes searched around the cave.

Billy followed her gaze into the shadowed recesses, an uneasiness creeping into his thoughts.

'I need you all to listen, carefully,' announced Ameer. 'There are forces at work on Aridian, the like we have never before encountered. Not only is our world in danger but the future of other distant places and other peoples is also under threat. The powers of evil have arrived amongst us and are already preparing to overthrow and enslave us all. We have to mobilise our armies and defend our people against a great and terrible adversary. We must send out the falcons to alert our communities.

'There is to be a meeting of the Sisterhood at Arachnae and we are to make haste there ourselves, gathering those that we need along the way. Billy, you shall ride with me. I have a message from Cassaria that I must deliver to you once we have begun our journey. Frog, you shall ride with Nadiah.'

Billy gave a quizzical look at Frog who shrugged his shoulders in return.

During the meeting with Cassaria two events had stuck in Frog's mind. The first was that she had asked him for a teardrop, explaining that she would use it to create a protective spell for him, in the same way that she would use the one taken from Billy earlier. And so he had allowed her to evoke a sadness spell on him. A single tear had welled up and tumbled down his cheek, which Cassaria had gently caught in a small glass vial. The second thing was that she had then spent some time with Ameer in her private room where they had shared a hushed conversation. Frog could also not guess what information was to be passed on to Billy and how he was to be involved. He was, however, intrigued and – dare he admit it – a little jealous of his friend as they all set off in procession up the wide passageway to the surface.

Meanwhile, two unseen reptilian eyes looked down from the shadows high above them and absorbed the scene before their owner finally sensed the air with its moist, flicking tongue. Then, silently, it turned and made its way back into the passage that it had hewn down from the surface to infiltrate Aridian's tunnels.

The party reached the tunnel entrance and passed out into the moonlight. Frog noticed several guards perched high on the surrounding rocks, their eyes alert and searching the surrounding dunescape.

Ameer brought the group to a halt and called to Nadiah who quickly dismounted the Sandspider, leaving Frog to sit alone. He watched curiously as she and Ameer walked to one side away from anyone's earshot. Ameer did all of the talking, as if issuing instructions, whilst Nadiah nodded several times to confirm that she understood.

Probably a message from Cassaria, he thought and then he turned his attention to watch several of Ameer's riders as they collected desert falcons, which were tethered to perches just inside the cave. Frog took in their splendid grey-white plumage, which gave them a ghostly appearance in the moonlight. He recalled that these wonderful birds could pursue their prey at a tremendous rate, often achieving speeds of over 120 miles an hour, making them the fastest of all living creatures. He watched as their handlers gently stroked the birds and spoke quietly to them, finally attaching a small roll of parchment to their legs.

Nadiah returned and took her seat in front of him on the Sandspider.

'What are they doing?' he asked her.

'Sending out information to the crystal farms and to Pelmore and Arachnae. They are very intelligent and loyal birds. During their flight, if there is something amiss, they will alert the falconers with shrill calls on their return.'

The falconers brought their birds into the open and, as one, they raised their arms and set the birds into flight. As the winged silhouettes disappeared out into the pale horizons, the group of Sandspiders and their mounts began their own journey out into the featureless desert landscape. The soft rhythmic drum of the spiders' feet was the only sound to betray their presence as the convoy wound its way across the sand.

As they progressed, Frog noticed that Ameer and Billy were deep in animated conversation as they rode atop their Sandspider. He asked Nadiah what Ameer had told her.

'Just messages,' she replied.

'If it concerns Billy, then it concerns me.'

'There are some things that you need not know at the moment – those are Cassaria's instructions,' explained Nadiah.

Frog decided not to pursue the matter and chose to use his time once again trying to communicate with his friends on Castellion, but to no avail.

They had been travelling for nearly an hour when, as they were halfway along a channel between two long and high sand dunes, Ameer raised his hand and signalled for them to come to a halt. The hairs on the back of Frog's neck rose as he sensed something was about to happen and his hand instinctively reached for his sword. At the same time, the riders drew their own long, curved scimitars. The blades slid silently from their sheaths to be bathed by the light of the over-hanging moons.

Nadiah turned and spoke to Frog. 'Whatever happens, do not get separated from me ...' she said, but a piercing howl cut off her words and more than twenty bodies materialised up from the surrounding sand, shaking the fine dust from their camouflage.

'Dreden!' she shouted at Frog.

Frog felt the draught of an arrow as it passed by his face and he turned to follow its path. He grimaced as it sank home into the neck of one of the riders. An unnatural gust of wind in the otherwise still night air picked up a cloud of sand and hurled it at the group, causing a moment of distraction. In those brief seconds, there was screeching everywhere. Dust and sand spiralled around them, their visibility reduced to less than a metre.

Frog felt the Sandspider lurch forward and a hand grabbed his robes, pulling him down onto the sand.

'Something is wrong,' shouted Nadiah into his ear. 'Dreden don't attack like this, not with cold-blooded killing. We have to get away from here.'

'We can't leave,' Frog shouted back. 'We must stay and fight.'

'There is a time for fighting and a time for running,' she yelled in his face. 'Now is the time for running.'

She pulled him away from the shelter of the spider and out into the swirling dust and sand, which scratched at his face and caught in his throat, making him cough. Nadiah's hand then found his scarf and pulled it over his head, wrapping it around to make a mask.

The dark shadows of the spiders loomed around them and the sound of steel on steel filled the air. Among the shouts of anger and pain, Frog heard Ameer's voice rallying his men, calling them to his side. Small pockets briefly cleared within the dust storm giving them glimpses of their surroundings. A body lay in front of them and Frog was thankful that it was face down as he stepped over it.

'Billy! Billy!' he called, now desperate to find his friend, but there was no reply.

The dust cloud closed in around them again and the wind whipped and tore at their bodies. Nadiah screamed and Frog turned to find that she was no longer standing beside him. He brandished his sword in an arc as he frantically turned this way and that, his eyes slits against the stinging grains of sand that assaulted him.

'Billy! Nadiah!' he shouted in desperation, then he heard a cruel voice in the distance.

'Find the boy,' the voice commanded and Frog turned again to see a dim shape bearing down on him. He crouched and swung his sword as he rolled to one side and felt the blade make contact. There followed a loud curse of pain and the figure dropped to the ground. Peering to his right he could see the dark bulk of a spider and he reached out and touched its hairy form, feeling for the leather strapping and quickly finding it. He grasped hold of the harness and pulled himself up until he was in the vacant rider's seat. Higher up now, he could see clearer areas in the dust cloud, which revealed bodies lying on the ground, some with dark red patches seeping through the robes.

Panic rose in him and he shouted recklessly. 'Billy! Nadiah! Ameer!' All he heard in reply was a swish followed by a dull thud as an arrow struck the Sandspider and embedded itself into its side. It reared up and gave an ear-splitting scream of pain. Frog lost his grip and slid sideways down on to the sand, the impact knocking the breath out of him. As he lay there a new horror gripped his senses: the sand was sinking beneath him, pulling him down as if into a funnel. He scrabbled with his remaining strength, but unseen hands wrapped themselves around his arms and legs, speeding his decent into the smothering, claustrophobic hollow that was engulfing him. He took in one last breath and closed his mouth and eyes as he stretched an arm out above him in desperation to grasp a lifeline, but his clawing fingers felt only sand as it sealed above him to complete his burial.

In the desert storm that had descended on them, Ameer and his men used their lifelong skills to defend themselves and cut down their attackers. Then, as quickly as it had appeared, the sand storm dissolved to reveal over a dozen Dreden bodies strewn around. The assault had only lasted a few minutes, but the intent was not that of a normal raiding party; this was the most vicious attack that Ameer had ever encountered. One of his men was dead, killed in cold blood, and three of their spiders were injured through arrow fire. Normally, in any skirmish, a warning was given or a challenge was announced before the Dreden raiding parties attacked and usually the fighting was at close quarters; crossbows were only used for hunting. Swordsmanship and hand-to-hand combat was the general rule of engagement. Everything was different this time.

Ameer surveyed the scene. 'And so the treachery begins,' he said to himself, but he was shaken out of his thoughts by the voice of one of his men.

'My Lord Prince, we have lost the young ones.'

8

Underground

In his mind he was still falling, but this was through soft white clouds, their cotton wool shapes gently brushing his body as he passed through them. Somewhere, a girl's voice was calling for him, pleading with him.

'Frog! Frog! Frog! Breathe! For pity's sake, breathe!'

Another female voice reached into his senses.

'Here, let me try,' she said and he felt hands lift him up. Without warning, there was a sharp blow to his back. He exhaled in surprise and his eyelids shot open as dry, coarse sand escaped from his throat. He coughed and rasped as he inhaled again, tears filling his eyes.

'Here, drink this.' It was Nadiah's voice and he turned to see her offering him a leather water bottle, which he gratefully took. The water tasted sweet and refreshing as it washed away the dry sand from his mouth and throat. He splashed a handful across his face and wiped the gritty residue away with the back of his hand.

'Better?' asked the other voice as he focussed his eyes in the soft crystal light. She was maybe eighteen or nineteen, dressed in the same orange robes as Nadiah and with the same small black spider tattoo on her cheek. Her eyes were dark brown to match the wisp of hair that escaped from her hooded robe.

He took another drink and looked around. He was in a small cave, the walls and floor of which seemed to consist of sand. In the ceiling, only a couple of metres above them, was a trap door with small trickles of sand escaping from its edges. He stared at it for some time, trying to make sense of his surroundings, then he saw a third girl crouched at the entrance to a small tunnel. She was also in her late teens, in matching orange robes, with a striking black spider tattoo on her cheek.

'What's going on? Where are we and where's Billy?' he asked Nadiah.

'We have to move quickly. We are to take you to Sanctuary. Everything will be explained when we get there,' she replied.

'I'm not going anywhere until I know what's going on.'

'We are in a network of secret underground tunnels,' explained Nadiah.

'And where is Billy?' he repeated.

'Everything that Billy has done and plans to do will be in vain if we do not get you out of here quickly and find our way to Sanctuary. If you care about him you will trust me until we are in a safe place to answer your questions,' she told him with a no-nonsense determination.

'I've been kept in the dark,' he said. 'And I don't like it at all. I do trust you, Nadiah, but if anything happens to him I won't rest, even if I have to cross all of the Dimensions to get revenge.'

The look in Nadiah's eyes softened. 'You must trust your friend to do what he feels is right. He is also here for a reason and he understands that he always has a choice. The longer we stay here the more danger he is in and the less time we have to get to Sanctuary where you will be told what is unfolding. Now, we must make haste.'

The tunnels were just high enough for them to run through with their heads lowered and their shoulders hunched. The girls led the way, carrying small crystals that illuminated the small chambers through which they were passing, each with trap doors in the ceilings and more tunnels that led off in other directions. Frog followed as instructed, but after quite some time he became impatient.

'How much further?' he asked, as claustrophobia seeped into his concentration.

'Nearly there,' replied Nadiah and Frog became aware that the floor of the tunnel was sloping beneath his feet and a cool draught of air chilled the sweat on his face. After another 10 metres the tunnel opened out onto a solid platform of rock. They were now standing on the edge of a circular shaft that housed a wooden lift cage and Frog could see that it was suspended by glistening, twisted ropes that reached up into darkness. The girls entered the cage and Frog tentatively followed.

'How high are we?' he enquired as he tried to peer down between the shaft and the timber floor.

'Don't worry,' said Nadiah and pulled a wooden lever.

The lift lurched downwards. 'We've never had an accident. Besides, if you fell from this height you'd be dead from fright well before you hit the ground.'

'And that's supposed to make me feel better?' he said as his hands tightened their grip around one of the wooden bars.

The cage bumped and creaked as it slowly made its progress down the shaft until, just as Frog thought that things couldn't get any more nerve-racking, they exited out into an open space. He looked over the side in alarm to see that they were now descending from the roof of a large cavern, still some 30 or 40 metres up, its galleries illuminated by clusters of the light-giving crystals. Below, orange robes busied themselves backwards and forwards and some glanced with curiosity towards the lift. It seemed that they focussed their gaze fleetingly on Frog in particular.

As they got closer, Frog could see that there was a group of about fifty figures practising moves and patterns, which looked like a cross between Tai Chi and Taekwondo. Frog watched with interest as it appeared to him that they were sparring with each other with such force that they should be making full contact, but somehow they managed to deflect the blows without actually touching their opponents.

A sharp jolt distracted him and he returned his attention to the thick ropes that guided their progress. As they neared the ground, two large stone counter weights rose up past them. He could see a series of pulleys feeding more ropes to a big water wheel, which was embedded in the cavern floor. Two more robed figures pulled at levers and the flow of water slowed, bringing the momentum of the wheel to a halt as the cage bumped firmly onto the ground.

Frog's manners overcame his desire to push himself from the cage first and he stood back and allowed the girls to exit, thankful that they were quick and breathing a sigh of relief as his feet touched the smooth stone floor. Before he had a chance to relax, two tall figures, whose orange robes bore embroidered black spider symbols, approached them. The first one pushed back her hood to reveal the kind face of a woman that Frog guessed to be roughly his mother's age.

'Welcome to Sanctuary my young friend. The council are waiting. Please follow us,' she said, turning.

They quickly crossed to a wooden door, which opened as they approached it. Both of the women stood back and allowed Frog to enter a brightly lit room. On a stone plinth in the centre of the room stood the Hourglass in its cradle, the grains of sand rhythmically falling through its narrow tube. The difference now was that the Rune Stone was firmly seated on the top of the wooden cradle.

On either side of the Hourglass stood two more women in the familiar orange and black robes along with Cassaria, who smiled gently at him, the hood of ice-blue robes now cushioned her electric blue hair.

'Cassaria!' he exclaimed. 'What's happening? Where's Billy?'

Cassaria approached him and knelt before him on one knee, placing a hand on his shoulder.

'Be calm, young Frog. Your friend has now found his part to play in the events that are unfolding. Billy has journeyed into danger in order to create a deception, which it is hoped will buy us valuable time,' she answered. 'He willingly agreed and understood the risk that is involved. He is not without guidance and the Magic of the Guardians is with him for his protection and to aid him through his mission.'

'I don't understand why it's been kept a secret from me,' said Frog.

'Until this moment, only Ameer, Billy, Nadiah and I were party to what I am about to reveal to you and to those who are trusted to be present here.'

Frog looked around him and saw that the door was now closed and only Nadiah and the two girls had entered with him.

'Belzecra has been busy with her vile Magic,' continued Cassaria. 'She already has spies within the ranks of Ameer's men and we are informed that she uses desert creatures to infiltrate our settlements and do her bidding. We must use our trust sparingly. Our enemies believe that this meeting is taking place at Arachnae and that the Hourglass and the Rune Stone will be there. They tried to take you as part of their plans, but we anticipated their actions and that is why we were prepared to rescue you and create a deception so that Billy could fulfil his role.'

'And what is Billy's role?' asked Frog.

'He has become you, dear Frog. In sound, manner and image and at this moment, the Dreden believe that the boy that they have captured for Belzeera is you.'

'But how?' asked Frog, bewildered. 'How can he be me?'

'You should know by now that the Guardians possess

many forms of ancient Magic; one art is that of duplication and Billy was given such a potion that enabled him to become your double, your twin if you like, along with instructions on how to carry out his deceit and play his part.'

A light bulb lit up in Frog's head. 'The teardrop! You used my teardrop; you've turned Billy into my clone.'

'He is your double in every sense except for his mind. He still controls his own thoughts and memories,' explained Cassaria. 'He still has his own free will.'

'But how will we get him back? How will we return him to being Billy?'

'Billy's teardrop, which I will use to change him back into his own image, but more importantly we must arrange for his rescue after he has had the opportunity to find out the extent of Belzeera's plans. We know that if she thinks that she has you in her possession, then she will focus her mind on obtaining the Rune Stone and the Hourglass. Until the time of confrontation, this must be the last and only time that they are to be in the same location as you. If she were to bring them together with one drop of your blood she would be free to release the monster that is Lord Maelstrom and then they will have the power to cross the Dimensions and control the past and the future.'

'What is it that makes my blood so special and why do the Rune Stones react to it?'

'That answer is hidden in the history of the Dimensions and only known by the Guardians of old. All we can do is play out our destinies and protect you with all the powers that we hold,' answered Cassaria. 'Until Belzeera and Lord Maelstrom are eliminated, you and the safety of the Dimensional worlds will be in peril. The Guardians now know that even the world that you call home, the Dimension that is Earth, is part of their planned conquest, now that Belzeera has learnt of its existence.'

Frog lowered his head; his eyes stared at the flat, stone floor. In that last sentence, all that he had been through in Castellion – his underlying conviction that everything to do with the Slipstream was really just a series of dreams, his adventurous attitude that had shielded him from the reality of danger and death – was swept away. He now realised that he could wake up as the boy Chris in his own world and the threat could still be real. The evil could still exist and come to consume him and everyone that he loved and knew. As his mind struggled with these thoughts, however, the effects of the Slipstream worked into his psyche once again, adding maturity to his young years, taking him past what remained of his teens and giving him a ripe, adult mind. He still looked the same personable teenager, but as he raised his head there was a calculating, steely gaze in his eyes.

'Tell me what needs to be done, in this world or the next,' he said.

9

The Camera Doesn't Lie

As the sand storm and the Dreden had descended on them, Ameer had pulled Billy down into the shelter of the spider's large shape. He had also given Billy a small glass vial.

'This is it,' he said. 'Drink it quickly and remember everything that I have told you. Moreover, know this, Billy; we will not desert you. I swear on Aridian's people, my people, that we will not forsake you.'

Billy stared at the vial. 'Oh, what the hell! I wanted an adventure,' he said and brought it to his lips. He swallowed the dark blue liquid and felt it slide down his throat like warm treacle. 'Mmmm! It tastes like chocolate,' he said, but before he could even lick his lips, his eyes rolled back and he fell into unconsciousness.

Ameer gently, but quickly, dragged Billy's comatose body out into the swirling sand storm and towards the Dreden voices that he could hear. He turned Billy over and pulled the turban cloth up to protect his sleeping face. As he did so, he could already see the Magic at work.

'May the protection of the Guardians be with you,

brave Billy,' he said. Then he turned and disappeared back into the gloom to join his men in fighting off the attack.

The combination of voices and the throbbing in his head eventually brought Billy to his senses. He shifted slightly as people do when they first awake and immediately he realised that his hands and feet were tethered. He turned again and coarse leather cut into his wrists. He exhaled a gasp as the sharp pain brought him fully awake. His eyes wide open now, he took in the interior of a small cave.

'Awake at last. That must have been quite a bump you got falling from that spider,' supposed a man who was rising from a group of other men seated around a small fire. 'Still, it made our job easier, but it's a shame that it robbed me of the chance to kill more Aridian scum.' His hand clasped around Billy's jaw and he brought his face close enough for Billy to smell the man's stale and rancid breath. His skin was dark and leathery. His eyes were as black as coal and he wore long, lank hair to match. Billy boldly tried to pull himself away from the man's stare.

'She said that you'd be a feisty one,' he laughed as he viciously tightened his grip and the metallic taste of blood ran along Billy's tongue, as it was caught between his teeth. He made no sound, but he could not stop the tears welling up in his eyes. Refusing to cry, he kicked out in defiance, his heel catching the man on the shin, and the sharp pain made him curse and release his grip.

'Why, I'll slice off those troublesome feet of yours and then we'll see how you kick,' he said, drawing his long curved sword, which Billy could see had a wickedly serrated blade, designed to cause maximum damage on its victims.

'Stay that sword!' shouted another voice. 'She will not be pleased with damaged goods and we will all suffer her anger for your spite.'

A taller man appeared and pushed the first roughly to one side.

'If you want to practise your swordplay go and pick a fight with the Aridians instead of with a helpless trussed up boy,' he challenged. 'Or maybe you would like to take your chances against me.'

'You will not be a captain for long,' retorted the other. 'You're too soft for the new world that she has promised us. We must fight with vengeance and show no mercy to our enemies.'

The second man drew his sword and straddled across Billy, almost protectively.

'We all fight for what we believe is rightfully ours, but you enjoy the suffering too much; you relish the agony and pain you inflict on others too easily. I still fight with honour and for my kinsmen. She does not own me. I do this for my right, not for hers.'

The moment passed in tension as Billy waited for the clash of swords, but it did not come and he was glad to see the weapons finally sheathed by both parties and the first man reluctantly move away. As the murmur of conversation resumed, the tall man knelt before Billy and studied his features for a moment before he produced a small leather bottle.

'Here, drink this. It is only warm cave water, but I'll warrant that you'll not refuse to swallow it.' He placed it on Billy's lips and the young boy drank gratefully and deeply.

'No need for such cruelty,' said the man as he inspected and loosened the bindings on Billy's wrists and legs.

'Thank you,' said Billy gratefully.

'Don't thank me for showing kindness,' he replied. 'The vile witch has an unpleasant use for you, I'm sure of that. She made it very plain how valuable you were to her plans. I'm just making sure that I carry out my orders without giving her reason to inflict her rage on myself. But believe this, if you cause trouble or try to escape I'll turn your keeping over to him.' He nodded back towards the first man. 'As long as you're kept alive he'll not worry about what condition he delivers you in.'

'Thanks for the advice,' said Billy. 'What's your name?'

'Baron,' the man replied.

'Where are you taking me?'

'To her, in her fortress, two days' ride from here.'

'I take it that you're talking about Belzeera,' said Billy.

'The very same.'

'What has she told you about me?' asked Billy.

'You ask a lot of questions for one who has no options.'

'Like most evil witches she tells lies. I'd just like to make sure that you know the truth about me,' said Billy.

'All I know is that you are responsible for her brother's false imprisonment and you are the

95

bargaining point that will give her the Rune Stone that will free him. In return for helping, she will give us the power to reclaim and rule Aridian. Then she will be on her way, back to where she came from.'

'That's a pretty impressive lie,' said Billy. 'Anyway, how do you know that you've got the right boy?'

'She has shown us your image. Every man in our hunting party had it burned into his mind by one of her unpleasant spells. Besides, this leaves me in no doubt that you are the one called Frog,' he said as he lifted Billy's bound hands and indicated to the shortened little finger on his left hand.

Billy stared at it in horror.

'What's the matter?' asked Baron. 'It looks like a fairly old wound. What troubles you?'

'It ... It ... It ...' stammered Billy as panic rose in his chest. 'It still brings back bad memories,' he finished, hoping that the explanation was good enough.

'Huh! When you lose an arm, like my brother Dre, that's when you need to complain.' He stood up. 'I think that we've talked enough. Keep the water bottle, but use it wisely. Once we're on our way, we won't be stopping for a refill.' Abruptly, he turned and left Billy to clutch at the bottle and stare at his finger. By a morbid curiosity, he was intrigued with the stump and examined it in more detail. Then, he pulled back the sleeve of his robe and examined his arm. No scar! He'd had an accident on his skateboard the previous year, which had resulted in six stitches in his arm, but now there was no sign of the injury. His mind was racing with frustration; he desperately wanted to see himself, to see his reflection in anything so that he could confirm the full extent of the transformation. He looked around him. There was nothing and then he remembered; when he had changed from his combats, he had checked his pockets and retrieved his mobile phone. He had rolled it into the waistband of his robes. He felt for a bump in the material; yes, it was still there. He could use the camera facility to take a picture of himself.

He hooked his thumbs into the waistband, but it was no good; whichever way he turned, he could not retrieve the phone. He brought his knees up and tried to jiggle the illusive phone out, but he was interrupted by a sharp voice.

'What are you up to?'

Billy froze as Baron rose from the group and came towards him.

'I warned you; if you try to escape I'll have no sympathy for you.'

'I'm not trying to escape,' said Billy hastily. 'I need to go to the toilet.'

Baron looked at him suspiciously. 'If you're wasting my time –'

'Honestly,' implored Billy. 'I need to go. Now!'

'Right,' he said untying Billy's feet and pulling him up. 'Over here.' And he led Billy to a corner of the cave.

'I can't do it here. Not in front of everyone.'

'There's no room for shyness. Just turn your back. No one can see,' said Baron impatiently.

'You don't understand. I need to – you know – sit down,' pleaded Billy.

Baron breathed out through clenched teeth. 'Right, I will let you have your privacy, but one false move and

I'll cut off your legs myself and to hell with the consequences.'

He escorted Billy out into the night, to a small alcove just outside the cave entrance, where he undid the binding on Billy's wrists and handed him a small bundle of dry leaf-like material.

'That's all I have. You'd better make the most of it. If it's not enough then you'll have to tear some material from your robes. I will be the other side of this rock and if you so much as stick your nose out without permission then I'll cut that off as well.'

As soon as he was out of sight, Billy unravelled his robes and retrieved the phone. He crouched down as low as he could and shielded the screen as he switched it on. The display lit up with its colourful menu and he checked its status. The battery level was good and everything looked normal except for two things: the time was stuck on 17.45 and there were no reception bars.

'Typical! Where's a network when you need them?' he muttered.

He scrolled through the menu and set the camera function, turning the lens to himself. He took two pictures and saved them in rapid succession.

'Hurry up,' shouted Baron. 'I'm not waiting for much longer.'

'You'll have to give me a couple of minutes,' Billy shouted back. 'Unless you want to wipe my bottom for me!'

That should delay him he thought as he scrolled to his picture file and clicked to retrieve the last image. He had to use all of his effort to contain a loud gasp, for there on the screen was the face of Frog staring back at him. He realised quickly how easy it was to use his friend's new name, but to know that he now looked exactly like him was very freaky. He looked at the image and prodded his own face curiously, lost in fascination.

'Enough!' shouted Baron impatiently. 'Come out now or I'll drag you out.'

'Just finishing,' replied Billy as he switched off the phone and tucked it into one of his socks. The lump didn't look very obvious in the pale light and as long as he wasn't searched he didn't think that it would be noticed.

As soon as Billy emerged, Baron led him back into the cave and rebound his hands.

'I won't tie your legs as it will be easier to move you around,' he said. 'But a word of warning – if you try to run you'll quickly realise that there is nowhere to hide. We are in the middle of open desert and there is no other shelter for miles. So save your energy and you will avoid any punishment. Now get some rest; we leave at dawn.'

Despite his best efforts to keep awake, Billy fell into a restless sleep until the sounds of conversation and movement awoke him. He rubbed the sleep from his eyes as Baron approached.

'Take a drink,' he said.

Billy did as he was told.

'You will ride with me. Three things to remember: keep your face well covered, hold on to your water bottle and only do what I tell you. Now, follow me.'

He led Billy out into the now-reddening horizon,

which announced the arrival of the two burning suns. The other men had disappeared around the large rocky outcrop and Billy was encouraged with a shove to follow them.

As he turned the corner he nearly froze with shock at the sight of four ferocious, giant, black scorpions that stood together; their enormous claws and the wicked stings on their tails filled him with dread. One looked straight at him, its nightmare head clearly displaying two front eyes and six smaller ones: three on either side, giving it panoramic vision.

Billy was in two minds as to whether he should run. He didn't care where; he just wanted to get as far away as possible from the terrible creatures. As if in anticipation, however, Baron grabbed him and pulled him towards one of the giant insects. Billy tried to resist with all his might and in the end, it took four of the men to manhandle him up onto the scorpion, but not before one of them had given him a painful punch in the ribs, which momentarily took his breath away. By the time he had recovered, he was placed firmly in a rough saddle with Baron seated behind him.

'Unfortunately some of my clansmen do not possess the same patience as I.' Baron's voice sounded almost apologetic to Billy. 'I take it that you don't like our pets?' he said.

'I don't even like them when they're a normal size; they give me the creeps,' confirmed Billy.

'You'd better get used to them; you're going to spend a lot of time in their company for the next two days,' said Baron and pulled out a whip, cracking it over the scorpion's head.

The ride was bumpy and uneven as the creature scuttled across the sand with astonishing speed, holding its great claws out in front of it as though they were ready to slice into the very sky itself. The rush of air as they moved forwards gave welcome relief and somehow cooled the effect of the burning sun on Billy's robes. He thought back to the moment when he resisted the offer of the costume, but now, as all but his eyes peered out from his turbaned head and masked face, he appreciated Ameer's persistence.

There was no conversation and Billy was glad of the opportunity to gather his thoughts and reflect on what had happened to him since he had crept up on his friend in the garden back home. For all his bravado, he was wondering how this adventure would end and how he would return to his family who he dearly loved. He was even missing his young sister.

The shout of 'Hawk!' brought him out of his thoughts. One of the men was pointing to the silhouette of a bird hovering high above them and another man quickly produced a crossbow. With practised ease, he loaded an arrow and fired it at the target. Billy watched in horror as the arrow appeared to pass through the bird. Its shape buckled and it plummeted earthwards. There was a shout of triumph from the bowman and Billy recognised that the voice belonged to the man who had been so cruel to him earlier.

'Why shoot a harmless bird?' asked Billy.

'Aridians use their hawks to spy on us. I'm surprised that this one found us so soon. We'll pick up the body and see what message it was carrying.'

Unexpectedly, however, as the bird neared the

ground, its wings spread from its body and it curved out of its death dive with only a couple of metres to spare. It swooped across the sand and shot towards Billy. As it passed overhead in a blur, two feathers floated downwards. Baron reached out and caught one of them and then instinctively, before he could be stopped, Billy reached up with his bound hands and grabbed the second.

'Keep your trophy,' said Baron, holding his feather up to the sky before pushing it into the folds of his robe.

Billy craned his neck to see the hawk pump its wings and speed itself towards the horizon. He had a feeling that somehow the bird had played out exactly what it had been sent to do and that it wasn't an accident that he was in possession of the feather. He gently tucked it into his robes, sensing that it contained a message for him.

After the skirmish, Ameer had led his group back to the refuge of their base. He now knew that their plans had somehow been overheard as Cassaria had predicted, but he was both worried and puzzled as to how this could be. Was there a traitor among them? He found this difficult to believe, as all of the men that he had chosen in his group were well known to him. However, the Dreden had discovered the route of their journey and the result was the death of a comrade and three spiders injured. He would guard future actions and only release details to those that needed to know them at the last moment.

It had been two hours since the hawk had returned and its handler spent a few minutes stroking it reassuringly and checking that it was unharmed. He then confirmed to Ameer that it had delivered its messages.

Ameer gathered his group together and announced that as soon as new spiders were ready, the group would be leaving on another mission and that he was introducing the code of faith: no one would be informed of their destination or its purpose; they were to follow his orders without question and without council. If any of them wished to be reassigned then now was the time to step forwards. They had seen in the death of their comrade that new levels of danger had been reached and a cold and determined enemy had emerged. He could not guarantee their safe return. There was a long silence, but not one man stepped forward.

10

The Sisterhood

'We need you to seek out a man called The One. The Guardians believe that he has more than a small part to play in the current events here on Aridian,' said Cassaria to Frog.

'You mean that he can help us against Belzeera and Lord Maelstrom?'

'We are not sure of his final purpose,' said Cassaria. 'His presence has also been something of a mystery until now. It has been several years since rumours of his existence reached us. Some believed him to be an Aridian priest of the old order who grew tired of our underground society and chose to become a recluse, others deem him to have a more ominous purpose, but one thing is now clear: you must meet him.'

'You want me to go searching around in caves and tunnels for some strange person and you're not sure whether he's good or bad?' said Frog.

'Yes.'

'Here we go again,' said Frog, remembering his adventures in the Labyrinth searching for the Earth Sage on Castellion.

'We don't expect you to go alone,' added Cassaria.

'You will be accompanied by Nadiah and two of her best girls from the Sisterhood.'

'I'll be happy with just Nadiah, thanks.' But as soon as he had said the words, he knew that he had been too abrupt and to confirm his thoughts one of the women moved forwards.

'I had heard many things about the one called Frog,' she said. 'But ignorance was not a trait that was mentioned. The Sisterhood, whether young or old, are ready to fight and die if necessary to protect Aridian and the Dimensions. The girls that you so easily dismiss have been trained to defend our crystal farms with their skills. They are also no strangers to conflict and danger.'

'I didn't mean any offence,' he pleaded. 'It's just that I don't give my trust away easily and there is still a lot that I don't know about Aridian; for instance, what exactly is the Sisterhood?'

'We place our trust in you through the influence of the Guardians,' said the other woman. 'If you need proof of our loyalty and ability then come with us now,' and she swept past him, closely followed by her companion.

Cassaria placed a gentle hand on his shoulder. 'You must realise that these are a proud people. They do not yet fully understand why they need the help of a boy to fight their enemies, nor do they fully appreciate the depth of the evil, which faces us. Go with them and discover how the women and the girls of Aridian have learnt to deal with the constant conflict in their world.'

As they moved out onto the cavern floor, Frog observed that all of the women had the spider insignia on their robes and that everyone had the delicate tattoo on their cheeks. They passed one group that was sparring and exercising. Then they came to a circle of a dozen girls. Each one of them had a pile of what looked like small, coloured beanbags at their feet. A short-haired woman at the centre of the circle stopped addressing them to acknowledge Frog and his escorts.

'Girls!' she exclaimed. 'We are honoured with unexpected guests.'

The group turned their attention to Frog and some of them audibly questioned the presence of a boy in their midst.

'Quiet! We have one of the Sisterhood's brightest stars amongst us. Nadiah, would you take my place and demonstrate your skills?' she continued.

Nadiah looked at the two accompanying women who nodded in approval. She then moved to the centre of the circle and Frog noticed the same quick hand movements, in and out of her robes, that she had made before demonstrating her skills to Billy. She closed her eyes and took in a long, slow breath as she lowered her head and dropped her arms by her sides, her hands clenched in fists.

'Ready,' instructed the woman and the surrounding girls picked up two bags, one red and one black, in each hand.

'Red!' she shouted and one after the other, the twelve bags flew at Nadiah, all aimed at her upper body and head. As the first bag was released, Nadiah's eyes shot open and before Frog could take in a breath, she had swept out her arms and the bags were deflected in mid-air to ricochet back at the circle of girls, some of whom needed to duck or dodge the speeding objects. Nadiah regained her relaxed pose and accepted excited applause from the group.

'Now with the hood,' directed the woman.

Nadiah pulled the hood of her robe down over her head to conceal her face. She then positioned her arms at her sides. This time Frog observed that a faint glow emanated through her closed hands.

'Black!' snapped the woman and the remaining twelve bags were thrown simultaneously. Nadiah dropped her body and swept one arm around her in a circle while her other arm shot straight up, the wrist twisting in an almost impossible rotation. Not one object reached her. All of the bags struck an invisible barrier and fell to form a perfect circle on the ground around her.

This time the applause was ecstatic as she stood and pulled back her hood to reveal a beaming smile. Frog clapped enthusiastically as he walked forwards to congratulate her, drinking in her smile and not understanding why he felt a tingling sensation in his stomach and chest. He nearly forgot himself and hugged her, but restrained himself at the last minute and murmured, 'Brilliant,' as he patted her on the shoulder instead.

Suddenly, shouts of alarm filled the air, mixed with screams of urgency. As one, all of those on the cavern floor turned their faces upwards, their expressions turning from apprehension to disbelief as a black shadow spilled out from the lift shaft above and spread like a stain across the ceiling. Dark shapes detached themselves to free-fall towards the ground in a sinister downpour of squirming insect bodies.

Cassaria was the first to react. 'Sanctuary is breached! Defend! Defend!' she shouted.

Frog watched as the initial chaos evolved into a disciplined action. Groups formed across the floor, a circle of orange robes shaped itself around the edge of the cavern, immediately reinforced and swelled by throngs of the Sisterhood from the tunnels and lower galleries.

The first of the scorpions – at least a metre long, its sting glistening with green venom – dropped to the floor and charged at the edge of the circle. Many arms rose in unison and Frog stared open-mouthed as an invisible force hit the creature and it shattered into a mass of black and green pulp. As he looked around, he saw battles in all directions as more and more of the oversized intruders poured through the opening, threatening to overwhelm all who stood in their way.

Some of the Sisterhood on the higher galleries fought desperately, but the venomous stings found their marks and orange robes crumpled to the ground. Frog had to turn away as he saw one unfortunate figure overpowered by three of the creatures, their pincers tearing into the orange robe as it disappeared beneath them.

Cassaria turned and gathered Frog, Nadiah and the two girls to her.

'We must put as much distance as we can between the Rune Stone, the Hourglass and yourself. I must now secure them to a far safer place and you must start your quest with urgency. I don't suspect that Belzeera knew of this particular gathering; this is just one of her random attacks to test our strength, but for now you and I have separate roads to take.'

Four scorpions broke through the ranks behind her and scuttled with unnerving speed towards them, their pincers raised, scything the air, tails arced, the hooked stings poised for attack. Frog drew his sword and the blade flared a blue-white light as he clasped it with both hands in front of him. Nadiah and the two girls moved to either side, their clenched fists glowing with unseen power, and Cassaria turned to face the oncoming menace.

The scorpions separated, three broke away to attack Frog and the girls while the other remained focussed on Cassaria.

Suddenly, the creature threw itself forward, its head and claws flattening onto the ground as the tail rose up and whipped towards her. She stood her ground and an unseen wind billowed her hair and robes around her. She then raised her arms and the bangles blazed gold. The sting came down in a deathly curve and she caught it impossibly between her wrists, inches from her face. Trapped in her grip, the tail ignited in a white-hot flame and as Cassaria stepped back, the creature burst into an inferno, its whole body writhing and shrivelling before finally collapsing into a pile of smoking charcoal dust.

As this happened, the girls directed their attention to two of the other attackers. The unseen force from their fists blasted the black bodies, which dropped dead in their tracks. The third creature leapt at Frog, who twisted sideways and with a curving slice of his

109

sword, he removed its head and one of its claws; black liquid spilling out and covering the cavern floor.

Cassaria shouted above the echoing cacophony of noise.

'You must leave, now! You know where your journey starts, Nadiah. If you succeed then we shall all meet again at the place of reckoning.'

Then she turned with a swirl of her cloak and they watched as she advanced towards the black, writhing mass. She raised her hands and again brought her wrists together, the gold light building into a blinding glare. Once more, she turned her face back towards them.

'Go! We must make sacrifices to win this battle and you must not be among them. Now go!'

Nadiah dragged Frog to an arched alcove where she pressed a small carving in the rock and a door slid gently away to reveal an illuminated passage into which they all hurriedly stepped. A wave of light and heat exploded out in the cavern and it rushed towards them, reaching the narrow gap as the wall slid silently back to block its progress. In a moment of darkness, a deathly silence surrounded them.

11

Caught in the Middle

The rest of the day's journey passed without incident, but for Billy it was an uncomfortable ride and the heat caused him to doze off now and again into troubled dreams, only to awaken with a raging thirst. As much as he had tried to conserve his water, he only had a couple of mouthfuls left and as the crimson suns melted into the heat haze of the horizon, he wondered if they would continue to travel through the night. He had lost all sense of feeling in his bottom and the onset of cramp was beginning to appear in his legs. Long shadows from distant dunes stretched out across the desert floor and he could see no sign of shelter.

'Will we be stopping for a rest?' he enquired.

'Soon,' was Baron's short reply.

Just as darkness enveloped the landscape, Baron tapped the side of the scorpion's head with the handle of his whip and the creature slowed its pace and turned towards a nearby sand dune. As they approached it, Billy noticed a gully opening up and sloping down into the mound. As they drew even closer, he could see a large entrance. They progressed down the sloping channel and into it, passing two Dreden guards, and as they did so, the enormity of the structure became clear. It was a false dune made of sand-coloured material, which was supported by a wooden frame that gave it a dome effect. Billy was impressed by its camouflage and the sheer size of the construction, which housed at least a dozen more giant scorpions. From what he could see, it also stationed over a hundred men.

As he was lifted down from his seat, pins and needles attacked his legs and he found himself dancing a jig, trying to get the circulation working again.

'What foolery is this?' asked Baron.

'My legs have gone to sleep,' Billy explained.

'Get moving. I'm hungry and in no mood to put up with your antics,' he ordered.

Billy hobbled over to a rough blanket on the ground and Baron ordered him to sit on it. He then retied his hands to a long leather tether, which was fixed high up and well out of Billy's reach. Baron checked Billy's wrists, examining the redness from the bindings.

'I'll bring you some salve to take away the soreness and you'll get some food shortly.'

'Thanks. Any chance of some more water?' Billy asked hopefully.

'I'll see what I can do,' he replied taking the water bottle.

Billy noticed that the man who had previously threatened to cut off his legs was staring at them.

'What's that nasty guy's name?'

'Zebran. You don't want to go tangling with him,' advised Baron. 'That witch has brought out his real evil streak. He was ruthless enough before she got into his mind, but now he tests even my resolve and patience with his cruel ways.'

He rechecked that Billy's tethers were secure then moved towards a small group of men, who were distributing food to the newly arrived group. After a while, he returned to place a wooden bowl into Billy's lap, containing what looked like Atemoya and strips of dried beef. He placed the water bottle on the ground at Billy's side.

'This is the all water you will get until we reach our destination tomorrow. Make it last.'

Billy looked down at the food.

'Is this what I think it is?'

'Dried Serpens and Atemoya,' confirmed Baron.

As much as Billy's mind told him that he could do without the food, his stomach ached with hunger and he resigned himself to the necessity of having to eat it.

'How am I going to eat?' he said pulling at the tether.

'I will free one hand, but do not try to untie the other. There are many eyes on you and most of them would not think twice in bringing you down with an arrow should you try to escape,' warned Baron as he released Billy's right hand.

Billy was left alone to chew on the salty strips that this time reminded him of pork crackling, and with a few sips of water, he managed to satisfy his hunger pangs.

As he ate, he watched the Dreden assemble and hold a discussion that, as it progressed, became more and more heated. At first, he couldn't hear or understand all of what was being said, but one person kept giving him piercing and hostile stares. Zebran would then

113

turn back, raising his voice and leading others in vocal aggression. There was obviously some kind of power struggle taking place and it became clear to Billy that some of the group had not fallen entirely under Belzeera's spell, while others were more faithful to her; a dark hatred had welled up in their hearts and minds and they thought nothing of slaughtering the Aridians and of the rewards that she had promised.

'We should have killed them all,' shouted an angry voice.

'Our orders were to capture the boy – nothing more, nothing less,' said Baron.

'If we are to take back Aridian then we must rid ourselves of our enemies at every opportunity,' challenged Zebran. 'You have become weak as a leader and have no loyalty to our cause.'

Baron gripped the hilt of his sword and spoke purposefully.

'My loyalty is to the Dreden, not to Belzeera. I will follow her as long as she takes only what she needs and leave us with what is rightly ours, but I will not kill for the sake of killing. She may have brought hope to our cause, but it would be purchased at a terrible price if we allowed ourselves to do her bidding at every turn.

'Our part of the bargain is to deliver the boy. Once she has him she will take the Rune Stone and her vile army and leave us with the power to defeat the Aridians so that we will have the freedom to roam wherever we desire. Those of you who wish to join her can do so, but my future and that of all true Dreden lies here on this world.'

Zebran changed the tone of his voice. 'Of course, we

114

could have supremacy over both our own world and that of others should we take the opportunity. They say that the boy's blood is the link to the power. If we bring him and the Rune Stone together, then we will not need the witch. It is we that should be the rulers and conquerors.'

Many of the group now saw the possibilities and voiced their support for him, the sudden prospect of power and unknown rewards fuelling their greedy imaginations. Zebran saw that he now had the majority of the support and seized the opportunity that he had waited for for so long.

'I will lead us to the victory and the power,' he shouted and leapt to his feet, drawing his sword. 'We shall take what is rightly ours and more, without mercy, without bargain.' His face seethed with venom and rage.

His followers took his lead and brandished their weapons. Amidst momentary chaos, the two groups divided and faced each other. Zebran, wild eyed and thirsty for blood, taunted Baron.

'You are feeble minded and stuck in the old Dreden ways. A new dawn has come and there is no place for weakness. You and what is left of your followers must bow to my command and join us or you will die here at my hand.'

Baron and Zebran stared at each other across no more than a metre of space. A hushed silence filled the air for what seemed an eternity and Billy held his breath. A small bead of sweat appeared on Zebran's cheek and Baron chose his moment. He brought his sword out and up from its scabbard. The blade swished towards Zebran's throat, but he was too slow. Zebran flicked his sword with practised ease and blocked the blade with a clash of metal. In that moment, all hell broke loose with men slashing and striking at each other. Billy looked on in horror as blood flowed and the reality of battle unfolded before his eyes. He tried to look away, but he was captivated and in those moments, the reality of his predicament hit him.

This is not a game Billy, Frog's words echoed in his head.

From the crowd of fighting bodies, one figure emerged and headed towards him. It was Zebran and he had a look on his face that sent a chill down Billy's spine.

'There is no mention that you have to be alive when your blood is spilt onto the stone and you will be less of a nuisance dead.' He smiled the words as he advanced, his already blood-stained sword raised to strike a fatal blow.

The sword scythed towards him and Billy could see from the trajectory that the intent was to separate his head from his body. He gathered all of his resolve and held his nerve until the last moment when he ducked his head down and stretched out his tied hand, so that the blade sliced through the tether. In that instant, he was free and snatching the water bottle. He rolled sideways, kicking out as he did so, and forced his heel into Zebran's leg. He felt it connect just behind Zebran's knee and he heard the screech of pain that followed. He didn't turn or look; he just forced himself onto his feet and ran as fast as he could towards the entrance, escape and survival the only thoughts in his mind.

The guards had left their posts to join in the confrontation and he passed unchallenged out into the chill, desert air. His feet pushed into the sand as he scrambled up the channel until he was faced with the vast expanse of barren wilderness. There was nowhere to hide, nothing that would conceal him from any pursuers and, more in panic than judgement, he ran around the edge of the false dune, hoping to buy himself some time in the shadows.

He stopped halfway around its circumference, his breath coming quickly as he tried to gather his thoughts. He then remembered the feather and the message that it might contain and felt inside his robes. The quill was a little dishevelled, but still intact. He stroked it with his fingers, easing the barbs back into shape, but he could not see any obvious markings as he turned it over and back. He held it up to the silver silhouette of a moon; it was then that the words appeared, the moonlight shining through the small plume.

TAKE COUNCIL WITH HE WHO IS
CALLED BARON.
HE WILL BE YOUR GUIDE.

Oh. Great, thought Billy. *Why didn't I look earlier?*
He stared at the message again, digesting the words. The reality of what he now had to do filled him with dread as he moved to make his way back to the dune's entrance and discover if Baron was still alive. His mouth was suddenly dry and he took a swig of the bitter, warm water from the bottle.

'Yuck!' he spat. 'If I ever get out of this alive, I'm never going to moan about warm coke again.'

The fearsome noise of fighting grew louder as he stealthily approached the entrance and he tentatively looked in. He could see bloodstained bodies spread out on the floor and quickly turned away to avoid seeing too much detail. Then, gritting his teeth, he looked again, this time focussing on the upright figures, searching for Baron. He saw Zebran suddenly limp out from a tightly knit group and with him half a dozen of his followers; they were heading in his direction – the only way out.

Billy stepped back into the shadows before he could be seen and waited as Zebran and his men bundled past. They were cursing as they made their way over the ridge and into the night, followed by half a dozen arrows, which fell short of their quarry.

He heard others approaching and he pressed himself against the side of the dune, desperately trying to melt into it. Two figures appeared, red-tinged swords glistening in the moonlight.

'I'll get some of the men and we'll run them down. We'll crush them like the insects that they are,' said a voice.

'They have nowhere to run except to her,' came Baron's voice. 'Whatever happens, I swear that her protection will not be enough to save the treacherous cowards.'

He sheathed his scarlet sword and with a movement so fast that it was a blur, his hand shot out and grabbed Billy's arm, pulling him from the shadows.

12

The One

As soon as the door sealed itself, Nadiah took four light crystals from a small alcove, each one attached to its own leather lanyard. She had hung one around her neck and the others had followed suit.

As they jogged along the tunnel, the crystals illuminated their passage while throwing out a myriad of shadows in their wake. Frog had lost track of the time as they journeyed, but the girls seemed tireless, never slackening their pace, except to halt for a few moments to drink when Nadiah uncorked a water bottle and passed it around. Each of them swallowed the refreshing liquid and then they were off again before Frog could say a word. He was trying to piece the events together in his head, knowing that asking questions would only delay them, but, ultimately, he knew that he would have to trust Nadiah's judgement.

The tunnel twisted and turned, but there were no junctions, no alternative paths, and the ground remained level. Frog deduced that wherever they were heading, it was certainly not back towards the surface.

After two further water stops, they reached the base of a short flight of stone steps, at the top of which was a large wooden door with heavy black hinges and a circular metal handle. Firmly seated across it, resting in two metal brackets, was a sturdy wooden beam. Nadiah stepped up and pressed her ear to the door.

'What can you hear?' questioned Frog.

Nadiah signalled for silence, as she pressed closer to the thick wooden grain. They stood in the eerie quiet, which was only disturbed by the sounds of their breathing. After a minute, she stepped back, concentration etched on her brow.

'I can detect no presence, but in these troubled times we must expect the unexpected. I will enter first, Frog will follow and – you two – be ready to pull back and bar the door should we need to retreat,' she instructed. 'Frog, help me lift the beam, but do so quietly.'

Frog stepped up and they lifted the length of wood from its metal cradles and put it to one side. Nadiah gripped the handle, ready to twist and pull the door open.

Frog drew his sword, its blade dazzling in the light of the crystals. Nadiah turned the metal latch and pulled the door slowly back. The light from their crystals pushed back the shadows into the awaiting chamber as Nadiah moved to the left, Frog to the right and the two girls stepped forwards to fill the doorframe.

Frog took in the scene. The seats and benches that filled the small auditorium were carved out of stone with a central flight of steps reaching up between them; there was seating for maybe a hundred, no more. A small stone dais occupied the centre of the floor.

'What is this place?' asked Frog.

'This was the first meeting place of our elders when

we retreated underground to escape the devastating change on Aridian's surface,' explained Nadiah. 'It was here that the first decisions were made governing our people. It was also here that the first opposition was raised and the leaders of those that were to become the Dreden announced that they were returning to the world above. They craved the sunlight, no matter how harsh it may be.' Her voice echoed flatly around the walls. 'There was much arguing and bitterness; families were divided, relationships and trust destroyed, animosity abounded. The old ones abandoned this place, as it held nothing good within its walls, no positive legacy for those who chose to remain –'

A dry scuttling noise stopped her and all four of them grouped in a semi-circle ready to meet any oncoming foe. Their eyes strained at the shifting gloom among the rows of benches and the two corridors on either side that receded into darkness. As they stood motionless, Frog's ears could only hear the tension in his breath. He wanted to break the silence; he wanted to shout, anything to provoke a reaction. Then, the dry rustle came again, to their left, three rows back. As they shifted positions, Frog saw Nadiah clench her fists and the familiar glow radiated through her fingers.

With a swift movement, she thrust her palms forwards. A shock wave rippled out, followed by a small whimper from behind the seats and then there was silence. She moved slowly towards the row of seats, signalling for the others to stay, but Frog instinctively covered her back, following close behind her and watching nervously as she climbed the short steps. As she looked between the seats, she gave out a gasp of surprise and reached down.

Frog could not see at first what it was that she cradled closely and protectively to her breast. Then, moving closer, he could see a small body, about the size of a large cat, wrapped amongst the folds of her robe. A paw hung limply from her hand as she made her way back down the steps. Finally, she knelt on the floor and the others gathered around her as she cradled the animal with open tenderness.

'Had I known, I would never have inflicted harm on her. I am only too relieved that my aim was to stun, not to kill.'

She gently allowed it to settle in her lap and Frog gazed at the animal. In the light of the crystals, its sleek red and brown fur flickered as if covered with small dancing flames, a brush of a tail curling over its legs, but what mesmerised him most was the size of its ears. They were conical and largely out of proportion with its body. The girls were equally transfixed.

'What is it?' he asked.

'Something that has not been seen amongst our people for many, many years. They have all but passed into legend,' replied Nadiah.

'Does it have a name?' he asked.

'They are generally known as Firefox, but I do not know what her individual name is,' she replied.

Frog noticed that her fingers trembled slightly as she absently stroked the animal. 'How do you know that it's a she?' he continued.

'Because the males have black ears.'

'Is it dangerous?' For some reason as soon as he had asked the question, he felt stupid.

'No, it is a seeker of truths for whomever it serves. It is a gatherer of information and it can sense deceit and lies. It can slip into rooms and places almost unnoticed to the untrained eye and it can direct its listening to the smallest of whispers. When it looks into your eyes, it sees your innermost thoughts and intentions.' She paused and looked at the Firefox. Her eyes moistened and a tear slipped down her cheek.

'They were persecuted by many after the great change that drove us from the surface. Some chose to shun them, then eventually they became so mistrusted that they were banished into the wilderness, passing into myth. The Sisterhood educate us in many of the old cultures, but as far as I know, there are none alive who have had the honour to meet or even see one of these beautiful creatures.'

One of the girls reached forwards to brush the coat with the tips of her fingers and at that moment, the Firefox's eyes opened. The effect on the girls and Frog was of raw emotion as they stared into its blood-red eyes.

In that moment, Frog understood why he was foolish to have asked if the animal was dangerous and a sense of concern for its safety welled up within him; he felt that he should protect it with his own life if necessary.

With tears of distress in their eyes, the girls were pleading for Nadiah to reassure them that the animal had not been harmed.

She spoke to it quietly and softly in a strange language, finally kissing the backs of its velveteen ears and gently placing it on the floor. It sat there on its haunches staring back at her and then it looked at the others, finally resting its eyes on Frog. It carefully stood on all fours and approached him, its beautiful eyes examining him intently. Then, it raised its snout and sniffed at the air before turning and scampering up the stairway, glancing back to them halfway up and raising its nose again as if to beckon them.

'We must follow,' instructed Nadiah.

Without question, they climbed the stairs and made their way through a small open doorway at the back of the amphitheatre.

The passage they followed was wide enough for them to walk, three abreast, and this time the ground sloped downwards. They walked at a brisk pace, following the bushy tail of the Firefox, the light of the crystals catching the sheen of its coat, which danced and shimmered like flames on the edge of the shadows. It moved briskly, never disappearing, but never letting them gain on it. Then, suddenly in a blink, it was gone.

'What now?' asked Frog.

'Shssh!' said Nadiah. 'Listen.'

Voices. The murmur of voices was ahead somewhere in the tunnel and Frog went to draw his sword. Nadiah placed her hand on the hilt.

'No. The Firefox would not lead us into danger. We are expected.'

Slowly, they walked forwards into a growing, stronger light until they turned a corner and entered a small chamber. A figure, its hooded cloak the colour of saffron, was crouched down and gently stroking the Firefox's ears. The animal licked an exposed hand then gave a sideways look at Frog before it disappeared through an opposite doorway. The figure stood and two dark hands folded back the hood to reveal the brown face of a man with chiselled features, a strong jawbone and broad nose. His hair was chestnut red with black streaks on either side. His voice when it came did not suit his appearance. It was gentle and soft.

'Sisterhood,' he smiled. 'It has been a long time. Far too long. Quickly, follow me,' he said, turning through the exit.

They followed along a short passage before they spilled out into a larger chamber where another cloaked and hooded figure sat on a large wooden bench. The Firefox sat before it and as they watched, the creature's coat shimmered and flexed. Its features grew and blurred until its form had changed into that of another tall, saffron-cloaked figure. Two hands extended from the cloak and threw back the hood to reveal a woman whose dark complexion blended into her long, flowing auburn hair, her deep red eyes and high boned cheeks complementing her soft red lips.

Frog's mouth hung open, not only because of the transformation but also because of her beauty. Nadiah saved him from embarrassment by gently lifting his chin and closing his mouth.

'Firefox,' she whispered, 'are changelings.'

Frog had just regained his composure when the woman spoke and the figure on the bench stood up.

'Frog, here is the one that you seek. We have guarded him for many years. You will know him by another name, but here on Aridian he has been known only as The One.'

The figure turned and pulled back his hood. The face that stared back at Frog was deep brown and careworn. A white scar interrupted the centre of his brow, but the man's features were unmistakable.

Frog opened his mouth and only one word could escape.

'Dad?'

13

Billy and Belzeera

Baron's men were already sorting through the bodies, tending to the living and removing the dead. Although Billy tried not to dwell on the scene too much, he noticed that far more of Baron's men had survived and very few were injured.

'I have a feeling that you are not all that you seem to be,' said Baron in a lowered voice as he took Billy to one side.

'What makes you say that?' asked Billy.

Baron leant forwards. He could feel the man's warm breath on the side of his face. 'I know that you are not the one known as Frog.'

'I … I don't know what you mean,' stammered Billy, unsure of how to continue.

'If I were to tell you that things are not always as they appear, what would that mean to you?' said Baron.

'I'd say that you were talking in riddles,' replied Billy.

'And I would say that you are very brave for a young boy.'

'I don't understand,' said Billy. 'Am I supposed to trust you or are you supposed to trust me?'

'A bit of both is required if we are to progress,' said Baron. 'Now, show me your feather.'

'Only if you show me yours,' said Billy stubbornly.

A smile came over Baron's face and he produced the quill. 'Come over to the fire,' he instructed.

As they crouched in front of the flames, Billy and Baron exchanged feathers and both held them over the firelight. Billy turned the feather in his hand and small writing appeared along the quill.

LET THE DECOY FALL INTO THE HANDS OF BELZEERA PROTECT HIM WELL

'I guess that my fate is in your hands,' said Billy.

Baron took the feather from Billy's hand and let it fall into the fire along with his, the flames engulfing them instantly as they disappeared in a flare of heat until no trace was left.

'Why did you do that?' asked Billy.

Baron glanced around them. 'There are still those amongst us who have not shown their true colours or loyalty.'

'And what is your loyalty?' asked Billy.

'To the future of Aridian and its people. We have lived in conflict for far too long and this witch will destroy us all if we allow her.'

'So, what's the plan?' asked Billy.

Baron studied Billy for a moment before he replied. 'I have not met the one known as Frog, but you do his name an honour. If he is to be measured by your bravery then he will have to do much to impress me.'

Just then, one of Baron's men appeared and, leaning

forwards, whispered in Baron's ear. Baron nodded and rose.

'We must leave,' he said. 'A group of my men are tracking Zebran and will do as much as they can to stop him from contacting Belzeera. Now, we must reach her fortress and create the diversion needed, so that those who work for the same cause of a united Aridian can bring the forces together to fight off the evil that has fallen upon us.'

Within minutes, Billy found himself reluctantly on the back of a scorpion again with Baron seated behind him. This time there were no bonds on Billy and the conversation centred on his approaching meeting with the witch and more importantly, his survival.

Baron told of the connection that he had with Cassaria and Ameer. For many months, he had been secretly working with them to encourage a meeting between the Aridian people and the Dreden in an effort to end the centuries of conflict when, suddenly, the threat of Belzeera had descended on their Dimension.

Billy's trust in Baron grew very quickly and he relayed the knowledge that he had learnt from Frog of Belzeera and Lord Maelstrom's plans to dominate and conquer the Dimensions.

As they talked, unwelcome ears took in their conversation. The scorpion that they rode was, after all, an instrument of Belzeera's making and its mind was at her command. It was not long before Belzeera became aware of their intentions and by the time they saw the silhouette of her fortress on the horizon, she had formulated her own plans and her dark preparations were ready for the unknowing pair.

The fortress towered over the desert landscape, a blood-red sky behind it heralding the rise of the oncoming suns. Either side of the opening stood gigantic burning braziers, the flames an unnatural mixture of green and orange. As the scorpion carrying Baron and Billy approached the gaping, ragged gap that served as an entrance, two enormous, grey lizard-like creatures padded out of the shadowed recess, their red tongues flicking out of their reptile mouths. Without a command, the scorpion lowered itself to the ground allowing Baron and Billy to dismount.

'I'll have to tie your wrists, otherwise it will look suspicious,' said Baron producing a strip of leather.

Billy held out his hands and silently allowed Baron to bind them. Again, he was struck by the seriousness of the situation. Frog was right; it wasn't a game and the danger was deadly real.

He looked up into Baron's eyes. 'I'm scared,' he admitted.

'That's good,' said Baron as he gave a tug of the bonds. 'She'll see it in your face and it will help to shield our conspiracy.'

Billy wasn't convinced. Suddenly, he wanted to go home.

One of the creatures let out a rumbling growl of impatience and raked its clawed foreleg across the ground, gouging deep track marks into the sand.

'Time to go,' said Baron and he gently shoved Billy forwards into the sickly haze that glimmered from the interior.

Baron had been to Belzeera's inner sanctum before when all of the leading clansmen were summoned there and she had infected their minds with her spells and the ambitions of Lord Maelstrom. However, Baron had found that he alone had heard her true desires to conquer and enslave all of them and release the dark evil that was her brother. He found the strength to shield his mind from her influence and vowed to unite the people of Aridian to fight against her and the menace that she brought.

He had so far been able to keep up the charade, but his confrontation with Zebran had exposed his loyalty and he was now in a race against time to complete Cassaria's deception to upset Belzeera's plans. He thought that the trickery was complete. He could not be more wrong.

Once his eyes had acclimatised to their surroundings, Billy took in the towering expanse of the citadel. The walls glistened and moved, the rock becoming molten disfigured shapes for a moment before solidifying again, constantly repeating the grotesque carnival across its surface, which disappeared upwards into an unnatural vapour cloud. A large rock-hewn staircase dominated the centre space and spiralled up into the mist. Billy looked behind him as the two lizards stood like sentinels blocking the way out.

'What now?' he asked.

'This way,' said Baron leading him to the foot of the staircase.

'Have you been here before?' questioned Billy.

'Yes. Now stop asking questions and get onto the step.'

Billy did as he was told and Baron stepped up beside him. The pale green mist cascaded down the stairs and settled around their feet. It rose above their ankles and spread out to quickly obscure any view of solid ground.

It took a while before Billy realised that they were moving upwards, following the curve of the steps, rising with the spiral stairway: a silent, eerie escalator taking them ever higher into the green, toxic-looking cloud.

As Billy breathed in the atmosphere, his head began to swim. It was as if his mind and senses were being poisoned, the bitter-tasting vapour stealing his compassion and reasoning, removing his morality and goodness.

When they finally emerged through the cloud and into the chamber that was more than 200 metres above the ground, Billy was under the total influence of Belzeera and Baron did not even know that the spell had been cast.

As the mist melted away to reveal a solid stone floor beneath their feet, Belzeera drifted out of the shadows to stop a metre or so away. Her voice was soft and calm.

'You have done well, Clansman, to bring the boy to me and by the look of him he is unharmed. Now I have another challenge for you. I want you to bring the Prince of the Aridians, the one called Ameer, to me.' She leant forward, her eyes staring into his. 'Dead or alive. Without a leader, they will crumble before us. Now, leave the boy with me and go.'

She stretched out her hand and an open doorway appeared in the wall behind Baron. He hesitated and put his hand on Billy's shoulder.

'As I risked all to capture him I would like to know of his future and learn of the Magic that he brings.'

Her hand flicked back towards him and in a blink, she held her black and twisted wand at his neck, the tip pressed into his skin. His throat tightened and he found it hard to breathe.

'Do not try my patience, Clansman. One twist of my wand and the only Magic that you will learn will be painful and torturous before your body and soul are swept away in a cloud of vapour. Now, go and do my bidding,' she scowled at him through gritted teeth.

Reluctantly, he backed away and down into the dark stairwell, leaving Billy to his own survival.

Belzeera watched Baron fade into the shadows and then she turned her attention to Billy who stood stock still, his eyes glazed and his skin pale.

'So, you are the image of the one they call Frog,' she said circling him and inspecting him with her cruel eyes. 'I sense there is a bond between you and he and that you are of his world. I'm sure that we can make great use of you. What say you, my brother?'

Again, her eyes rolled up into her head and Lord Maelstrom's voice came from her mouth.

'His blood will not serve the purpose that we need, but he will help us in our quest, my sister. He will be instrumental in my release and their downfall. He will bring the one we need to us, whose blood will open the Void. I will return with such a fury that all shall tremble and fall in my sight.'

Billy stood in a silent trance. Belzeera reached out to steady herself as the presence of Lord Maelstrom left her and her eyes returned to deep, black pools. She waved her hand and two stone seats slid silently out of the wall. She rested herself on one and motioned Billy to sit on the other. He did so with the mindless motions of a zombie.

'Now, my little friend,' she laughed softly. 'Let us see what secrets you hold. Let us test your fragile young mind.'

14

Revelations

Frog threw his arms around his father.

'I knew that you were alive. I knew it. I knew it,' he sobbed, burying his face into the folds of the man's robe. 'I've really missed you, Dad.'

The man put his hands on Frog's shoulders and gently pushed him back, his eyes searching Frog's face. 'You know me?'

Frog stared back. 'Of course I do; you're my Dad.'

The man's eyes searched again. 'Forgive me. I have no recollection of you.'

Frog turned to Nadiah. 'I don't understand. What's wrong with him?'

The tall, auburn-haired woman moved forwards. She took Frog's hands and clasped them around his father's.

'The ancient Magic of the Guardians nearly killed him and in the process it took his memory, but you have the power to restore it, young Frog. Now, place his hands on your forehead and let the light of The Chosen reach out into his mind.'

Frog looked down at his father's large hands and noticed the platinum wedding band that adorned the third finger of the left hand, a replica of the one that his mother wore and had always refused to remove. With her image in his mind, he leant forward and brought his father's hands up to his forehead.

A sudden, bright illumination of golden light spread from his brow and melted into his father's palms. The light was so intense that the others in the room had to look away and shield their eyes. They did not see the rich, yellow aura envelop his father and melt into his robes until his whole body shone with the radiance. Then, in moments, it was gone and Frog's father fell to his knees, his head bowed. They all stood around him, their eyes blinking in the pale light of the crystals.

Frog knelt down and lifted up his father's head. 'Dad? Are you all right?'

His father smiled. 'Hello son. You're full of surprises.'

For a few moments, the others stood in silence and witnessed the joy of a father's reunion with his son.

Finally, Frog spoke. 'Do you remember anything, Dad?'

'I remember more than I ever knew, including your adventures in Castellion.'

The woman stepped forward again. 'The power of The Chosen has not only restored your father's memory, but has also transferred the knowledge to him of everything that has happened to you since you came to the Dimensions.'

She held out her hands, helping Frog and his father to stand.

'Let me introduce myself. My name is Pasha and it was I who found your father in the tunnels long ago. He was badly injured and unconscious for many days and it took all of my skills to keep him from death's eager hands. I knew from his clothing that he was not of Aridian, but the two pieces of animal skin that he held in his hand eventually revealed the importance of his sudden appearance.

'He had no memory of who he was or where he had come from and so I took the skins and consulted with the Guardian Cassaria. She advised us to care for and guard him in secrecy. This has not been difficult as we have lived in isolation for many years and we have kept ourselves away from the conflict of the Aridians.'

She turned. 'This is Fray, my brother.'

The man moved to her side and took her hand. 'We are among the last of the Firefox,' he said.

'I can never thank you enough for saving my dad's life,' said Frog.

'It was meant to be,' said Fray. 'He is here for a reason. There is much to be said. So, now, let us retire for a while to surroundings that are more comfortable.'

They led the way to a softly lit antechamber, at its centre was a knee-high, wooden, circular table made from a cross section of an ancient tree. It was about 2 metres in diameter and surrounded by plain-coloured cushions. In a small recess, there were two, simple, raised camp-style beds and in another corner, there was clean, straw-like bedding.

While the girls, Nadiah, Frog and his father made themselves comfortable around the table, Fray and Pasha busied themselves, providing goblets of fresh water and bowls of fruits until they finally took their places at the table.

Frog sat so close to his father that the others thought

that he would dissolve into him. With his father's arm around him, the bond between them was clear for all to see.

'So,' said Pasha. 'Let us now hear about The One's journey to Aridian.'

'You don't have to call me that anymore; I know who I am now,' said Frog's father.

'All the more reason for secrecy,' said Pasha. 'Your son must remain as he is known in the Dimensions; his name is Frog, even to you and you must be known as The One to him and to all others.'

She produced the dried animal skins and placed them on the table. 'Somehow, these bind you both to the Dimensions and the evil that would return as Lord Maelstrom. Now tell us what you remember so that we can understand further why you have been brought here.'

Frog's father absently rubbed the scar on his forehead. He took a mouthful of water and then he recalled the events that had led to his arrival on Aridian.

'I was in a tomb that had been discovered a few kilometres from the Bou Craa phosphate mine in the Sahara desert. With a small team, I had been comparing the hieroglyphics on these ancient animal skins with those on the broken sections of a sarcophagus lid. No one had ever seen symbols or ciphers like it and I was still trying to recognise a pattern when I started to piece some of the lid fragments together. Then I noticed that the only symbol that appeared once on one of the skins and on a lid fragment looked like a door opening in a wall. That's when I had the idea of a hidden doorway in the tomb. We set to work examining the walls until eventually one of the Moroccan guides found the same symbol carved into a small single block of stone at the base of one of the wall sections.

'I was sure that this would operate the mechanism to open a doorway to another room. I placed my hand over the symbol and gave it a push. As it sunk back into the wall, we could hear the grinding and rumbling of moving rock. Dust started to fall from the ceiling and walls and we were about to evacuate the tomb, when the wall in front of us suddenly slid back to reveal a long dark passageway. Along its right-hand wall, another series of hieroglyphics were carved out in a line, which faded into the dark.' He paused for another drink, perspiration showing on his brow.

'It was decided that I would lead a small exploratory party into the passage and so, after equipping ourselves with torches and taking the animal skins so that I could continue to look for any translation, we moved slowly into the dark corridor. We had not gone far and were within shouting distance of the rest of the team at the tomb's entrance, when the shadows fell back to reveal another chamber. We were astonished at what adorned the walls. In striking pastel colours on the wall in front of me was a medieval scene, a castle with large flags flying from its turrets, each one decorated with a burning sun on a bright blue background.'

'Castellion!' exclaimed Frog. 'The sign of Castellion and The Chosen.'

'On the next wall,' continued Frog's father, 'was a desert landscape and hanging in the sky were two burning suns.'

'Aridian,' confirmed Pasha.

'To my left was the drawing of a tropical forest with a snow-peaked volcano standing in the background. I turned to look at the wall behind me, the one from which the passage emerged. It was painted with the view of a city landscape, skyscrapers and office blocks. There was an aeroplane in the sky above the scene. How on earth these images had been painted onto the walls of a Moroccan tomb was beyond me.

'I turned my attention to the floor in the centre of the room. A circle, large enough to stand in, was carved into the stone and within the circle were twelve symbols. I can remember kneeling in the middle of the circle, holding onto the animal skins. I matched all of the symbols in the circle to ones that were on the skins and I tried to interpret what they meant. I consulted Joe Stein, one of my colleagues who was with me; he also noticed that the same symbols appeared on each of the walls and we agreed on what we felt each one represented. We decided that while I shouted out each symbol he would try to locate its position on the walls.'

Frog could see the immense concentration and anxiety on his father's face as he wiped the sweat from his brow and recalled the final events.

'The first symbol that I touched and called out resembled a tree and to our amazement, the icon on the floor gave off a bluish glow as did the one on the tropical forest painting. The next resembled two fiery orbs and again when I touched it and shouted this out, the same image glowed on the floor and on the desert landscape. As I continued, various symbols illuminated on the floor and on the matching walls. I had just called out the seventh symbol, a spider, when the whole circle lit up around me, as did the desert painting. Cracks tore through the wall and jagged shafts of light burst into the room. The ground beneath me gave way and as I fell, I looked up only to see the roof caving in on my colleagues and a large piece of rock following me down into the hole and striking me on the head.

'I don't remember anything else from that moment until I opened my eyes to see Pasha leaning over me and wiping my face with a damp cloth. I had no idea who I was or what had happened to me.' He looked down at his hands, sorrow on his face.

'I lost some good friends and colleagues in that room and I still don't understand what really happened or why.'

'I can only tell you what was revealed to me by Cassaria,' said Pasha. 'You found an ancient gateway into the Slipstream. The secret of its existence was only revealed through an unforeseen shifting in the desert sands. It had remained hidden for aeons since last the elder Guardians, one of whom was buried at the site, had used it. The Guardians had many such gateways throughout the Dimensions; they used them to travel between the four Dimensional worlds to correct the balance between good and evil whenever evil threatened to become the greater force.

'The hieroglyphics were codes that, when used correctly, would open the Slipstream into each Dimension. A protective spell was placed on the gateway lest dark forces tried to use it and when you applied the symbols randomly, it triggered the spell designed to destroy the gateway and those attempting to use it. Sadly, those that were with you have perished and you would have also, but for some reason the Slipstream chose to draw you in and bring you to Aridian.'

Frog turned to his father.

'Look, I know it's sad that people were killed, but you were saved for a reason. I don't think it's a coincidence that we've been brought together in the Dimensions, especially since an old friend gave me some good advice when I first came on this crazy adventure. He told me, "Things are not always as they seem." And he's been proved right on several occasions. All I know is that I have been chosen to help stop some really evil people from taking over places that I never knew existed. Other people are prepared to die protecting me; in fact, some already have and I have to repay that sacrifice.'

His father studied Frog's face for a moment then he looked directly into his eyes and said. 'I cannot believe how you have suddenly grown in character since I last saw you. You're still my son, but you speak with such maturity and confidence. You're the same, but different. Does that make sense?'

'It totally makes sense,' said Frog. 'I'm two people. At the moment, I'm the one that they call Frog, but inside I'm still me, your son, Chris, and I can't think of anyone that I'd rather have here with me than you.'

His father looked down at his wedding ring.

'I only wish we were with your mother. I miss her so much.'

In the short silence that followed, a low howl echoed from the passageway.

'It's Jenna,' said Fray. 'Something's happening and she brings us news.'

All eyes turned towards the entrance to the chamber until another Firefox appeared. It ignored everyone else and went straight to Pasha who crouched down to let the animal lick her hand. She whispered gently to it and then stood back.

They all watched as the metamorphism unfolded again before their eyes. The animal's coat shimmered and flexed and then the human form took shape. A shock of short, deep-red hair framed the woman's dark face, brown eyes and small, pointed nose. As with Pasha, her lips were crimson red.

Fray introduced Frog and briefly told Jenna about the restoration of The One's memory, until finally Jenna spoke to them.

'I come from Cassaria with news and instructions. Sanctuary has been saved and the evil repelled, but at great cost. Many of the young students have been lost in the fight. If it had not been for her, then the loss would have been greater.'

One of the girls spoke. 'We must return to Sanctuary, Nadiah. We will be needed in the healing process.'

'The girls may return to Sanctuary,' said Jenna. 'They can make their way back through our safe passageways. However, your place is with us, Nadiah. Your future must be alongside Frog and The One. Say your farewells quickly as we too must leave to join another guarded assembly.

'Death and destruction spreads its vile shadow on the surface of Aridian and threatens the survival of all its good people. Sanctuary is not the only safe haven that it has infiltrated; we fear for the very heart of Aridian as the worst has now been realised. Lord Maelstrom has been released from the Void and descends upon us with a determined vengeance. His quest to invade the Dimensions and to enslave all who survive has been renewed.'

15

I am Released!

Belzeera had delved deep into Billy's subconscious; she had probed his memories and found much satisfaction in taking his mind to the brink of insanity. She had discovered many things about Billy's friendship with the boy who was now Frog; she knew how they had come to Aridian and she glimpsed his conversations with Cassaria, including the Magic of making him appear as Frog's double. She had also discovered the mobile phone hidden on him and she had learned of its use and function. She was particularly interested in its ability to capture images and while the body of a now deathly pale Billy lay on the floor, she proceeded to work her evil Magic.

She turned on the camera function and took an image of herself and then, retrieving the picture onto the screen, she placed the phone on the floor in front of her.

'Now is the time dear brother. Through me and the science of a Dimension yet to be captured, you shall be released.'

She then rolled up the sleeve of her robe and produced her wand. She pressed it onto the exposed skin of her arm, holding it over the mobile phone, her image glowing on the small screen.

'Come to me now. Use me as the channel to freedom.'

Her eyes rolled back into her head and Lord Maelstrom's voice boomed from her mouth, the ancient language of Dark Magic spilling out, resonating around the walls and quaking the very ground. Belzeera's hand involuntarily pulled the twisted wand across her arm and a thin line of blood ran along the flesh and dripped onto the small screen. A red mist poured out from the small illuminated panel and within the mist, an image formed. It morphed and shifted, the vapour turning into a tall, scarlet, billowing figure, until Belzeera stared at her mirror image floating before her.

Lord Maelstrom's voice boomed again. 'I ... Am ... Released!'

A jagged line of red-hot lightning streaked from Belzeera's mouth and into the shifting image that exploded. Fragments of it flew around the room until it slowly reconstructed its form and the atmosphere became still and eerily silent.

She smiled in wicked satisfaction as the figure stepped toward her.

'Welcome back, brother.'

His face was pale and bony and his red eyes held large black pupils. He was bald except for a long, black, plaited ponytail reaching down from the crown of his head and curling around his neck. The skin of his scalp was etched in black with the ancient runes of Dark Magic. His tall, wiry frame was clothed in a sickly green material that shifted

146

and glistened, a high-collared tunic framing his skeletal features.

'Sister, we have work to do,' he said and walked to Billy's body, which floated up into his outstretched arms.

16

The Council of Aridian

'All we seem to do is run,' said Frog as the group hurried themselves through the passageways. 'Isn't it time that we fought back?'

'There will be the right time for confrontation soon enough. The surface of Aridian is where our fate will be decided, but we must secure the underground communities and people of Aridian against any further assaults,' said Pasha. 'Cassaria has concerns that Lord Maelstrom's powers have increased and that we face the added threat of Belzeera's influence and presence.'

As they steadily made their way along, Frog became aware of a growing sound. At first, he thought that it was the noise of air rushing through the tunnels until, as they progressed, the noise became more urgent, more fluid. Then it was everywhere, the unmistakable sound of flowing, fast moving water.

They turned a corner and for a moment, as they all spread out along a stone platform, Frog just stood and stared. A large gully ran along in front of them, water rushing out of a tunnel on their right and disappearing into another on their left. Rattling against the platform as the water foamed and churned beneath them were four flumes made of a dark leathery material.

Frog looked up at his father. 'Somehow I don't think that this is going to be like the flume ride at Alton Towers.'

'Get in,' said Pasha joining Fray in one of the flumes. 'We must make haste. Black scorpions have been seen on these levels.'

'You and Nadiah ride together,' said Jenna. 'I'll sit with The One.' And before Frog could object, Jenna had bundled The One into a flume and sat behind him.

'Where are we going?' Frog asked.

'Arachnae, an underground city of Aridian. Now hurry.'

Frog let Nadiah climb into the second flume and then he sat behind her just in time as Fray pushed a lever to one side and the flumes jerked forwards into the tunnel, which was lit by rock crystals set into the dark, stone walls. The sound of water echoed around the tunnel as the flumes picked up speed and a gap of about 3 metres opened up between them.

'I hope that we're not going to get separated,' said Frog. 'I've only just got my dad back and I don't want to lose him again.'

'Don't worry,' replied Nadiah. 'There are regular basins that allow us to stop the flumes and get out to access various areas of our underworld or to carry on to another destination.'

After a while, they came to such a basin; it was a widened pool, alongside which ran a stone platform with an exit arch leading off from it. The three flumes regrouped in a line before Fray reached out and pushed back another wooden lever set in the platform and a small barrier swung away to let them continue their journey into the next tunnel.

'I wonder why Jenna wouldn't let me ride with my Dad,' said Frog.

'She has good reasons,' replied Nadiah. 'All Firefox have good reasons for everything that they do.' She turned her head to look at Frog. 'Am I to understand that you do not enjoy my company?'

Frog blushed. 'No... No... I mean, yes I do like your company. I think that you're great.'

She touched his hand and smiled. 'I'm glad. I like you also.'

Frog felt himself turn even redder. He was saved from further embarrassment by the tunnel suddenly ending and a wide-open cavern greeted them. They were about 50 metres up and travelling along a trough, which was suspended from the roof of the cavern by a network of thick, iridescent cables. Below them, he could see what resembled a collection of market stalls with robed figures, grown-ups and children going about their business. The whole scene was illuminated by some of the largest crystals that he had seen so far.

The flume unexpectedly shuddered as it bumped against the side of the gully and he instinctively grabbed hold of Nadiah to steady himself.

'Are you afraid of heights?' she asked.

'Not usually. I'm just not sure how safe this is, that's all. We have similar transport in my world but we use it for amusement and it is usually constructed of stronger materials.'

'We have never had any of our waterways collapse

and they have been transporting our people and goods for many, many years. You're quite safe, but I don't mind you holding on to me.'

'I will, thanks, but it's just to steady myself while we get across.'

Frog could not see the broad smile on Nadiah's face.

As they progressed, their speed increased from a leisurely pace to a more rapid one. They travelled in a more downward direction, the channels following twists and turns, until they came to larger caverns with a system of channels criss-crossing above and below them, all suspended by a myriad of supports and cables.

'How did they manage to build all of these waterways? I mean, it's a long way up for anyone to climb, let alone haul up these thick ropes,' said Frog.

'With the help of Sandspiders; the ropes are actually spider web,' explained Nadiah. 'Many, many years ago with the guidance of brave Aridians harnessed to their backs, the spiders helped to build most of the high constructions that you will see in our underground world.'

'And where do all of these waterways go?' asked Frog.

'Different communities, our plantations and store rooms,' replied Nadiah. 'Some of the channels feed the water wheels that take the water back up to storage tanks, which in turn keep the system flowing.'

'So how deep are we?' he asked.

'Deeper than you can imagine. It has taken us half a day to get this far since we left Sanctuary.'

'And how much further to go?'

'We reach Arachnae after the next cavern.'

Sure enough, as soon as they had crossed the following cavern and passed through a short tunnel, a large basin opened up in front of them. Frog could see that most of the water that carried them filtered away through drains set in either side of the channel, but not before it pushed them forwards onto the relatively calm surface of the basin. As they drifted towards the landing area, the others were being helped out of their flumes and Fray was already in conversation with a familiar orange and black-robed figure. It was Katar. He glanced a nod at Frog then turned his attention directly to Jenna and The One, to whom he was being introduced. Katar touched his forehead and bowed in acknowledgement.

Frog made straight for his father's side, not wanting to be separated a moment longer.

'Enjoy the ride, Dad?'

The last word echoed unnaturally. All of the others stopped talking and exchanged anxious looks. The pitch of the echo increased, as did the repetition of the word until it sounded as if someone inhaling helium had spoken it.

Dadadadadadadadadadadadadadadadadadadadadadad!

They all covered their ears, the volume threatening to burst their eardrums, until it finally exploded around them with one last deep, guttural, *DAD!*

His father crouched down, placed his hands on Frog's shoulders and looked him squarely in the eyes.

'Listen very carefully. Jenna has told me more about what has been happening here and how this Lord Maelstrom character wants to get his hands on you.

She has also explained that, even though it means twice the danger, you and I must now remain together. However – and this is going to be hard – from this moment on, we cannot, we must not, acknowledge each other as father and son. If the wrong people discover the bond between us, it will be our weakness and our downfall. It will bring catastrophe to this Dimension, which in turn will threaten the existence of our own world.'

Frog reached up and gently ran a finger along the scar on his father's forehead.

'I will call you whatever name is needed, but I will never cease to love you and I will never fear to deny who you really are.'

'You speak for both of us,' said The One.

Katar broke the silence. 'We need to leave this place. Let us now hurry to our destination and discover what future we play in the defence of Aridian.'

As they journeyed along the tunnels and galleries, Frog and The One marvelled at the underground city. They passed brightly illuminated caverns filled with varieties of green crops and a constant moisture hung in the air and glistened on the many, shaped leaves and stems. In other corralled recesses stood groups of the strange-looking Saurs. These creatures were about the size of very large dogs, but that is where the resemblance stopped. Their faces were similar to wild boars with curved tusks protruding from the corners of their mouths. Their deep-set eyes stared angrily from their brown, leathery and wrinkled faces. There were no ears, just small holes set in the sides of lumpy heads, which were too small for the rest of their bodies.

In the place of tails, there were stumps and their short, stubby legs ended in long clawed feet. Their whole bodies were covered in dark, tough looking skin.

'I wouldn't want to meet one of those in a dark alley,' commented Frog, which only seemed to provoke one of the animals into lunging forward at the barrier while emitting a half-bark, half-snort. 'I hope that they taste better than they look, 'cause if there was ever a good case for becoming a vegetarian, that's it,' he added.

The One gave him a sideways smile. 'I'm glad that you haven't lost your sense of humour.'

'I've learnt that life's too short to be without it, but there's also the right time to be serious,' said Frog.

'We are fast approaching one of those times,' said Katar standing to one side to let them pass through an archway onto a semi-circular platform. 'Behold the Elder Council of Aridian.'

The others spread out either side of Frog and The One. Frog noticed that Fray, Jenna and Pasha had all pulled their hoods over their heads and remained in the tunnel.

Before them, Ameer, Cassaria and two women from the Sisterhood stood in front of a group of twenty or so men and women dressed in various coloured robes. They did not look particularly old, but they all had silver-white hair.

Katar moved down and stood next to Ameer as Cassaria stepped forwards to address the gathering.

'Elder Council of Aridian. The circle of prophecy revolves another quarter turn and change has come to our Dimension. With it comes the spectre that is Lord Maelstrom, who is reborn from the Void with all his vileness. His sister, the witch Belzeera, aides him and has prepared the way for his ambitions to enslave us and to destroy all those who dare oppose him.' She moved towards the little group. 'Before you is the legend that is Frog and along with him, living proof that The One exists. They shall stand side by side with us in our defence.'

She turned towards Nadiah. 'The Sisterhood have already paid a heavy cost fighting back the evil menace. Even so, they pledge their young princess to the cause.'

Frog could not stop himself from gazing at Nadiah and would have continued to do so had she not stared back. Her eyes met his and for some reason, he felt guilty; he felt as though she had caught him doing something wrong and he quickly looked away, then he felt guilty again for doing so. He took a deep breath and looked back, but the moment had passed; Nadiah was now focussed on Cassaria.

'Now is a time for healing,' continued Cassaria. 'You must look to your past and those that you turned your backs on. As a Guardian, I protect all who stand for good and righteousness and so you must now embrace those that you deserted, for they have been in isolation for far too long and yet have continued to watch over you.' She raised an arm in indication. 'Welcome, Firefox.'

Fray, Jenna and Pasha stepped out of the tunnel, pulling their hoods back and exposing their faces. There were some gasps and murmurings from the assembly until Katar stepped forwards.

'These are among the last of the noble Firefox,' he

announced. 'Our shame is all the more that they forgive us for their exile. Know this, those of you that doubt them, they would still lay their lives down for Aridian and its people.'

Cassaria moved to one side, addressing all. 'There are others who fight for our survival. A young boy who is a stranger to our world and loyal to Frog has already put himself in grave danger. Many Dreden think that the time for reconciliation is long overdue; they too are secretly preparing to stand beside us and fight. You have only heard of news or rumours about the threat that grows above us. Let me show you why we must now act quickly and unite as one people again.'

She turned to face the wall behind her, raising her arms, and bringing her wrists together. The bangles gave off golden sparks as she pulled them apart, out and down until she had formed the shape of a circle in front of her. She stepped back for all to see the images that filled the circle.

Belzeera's stronghold dominated the desert skyline. Its tall, dark structure was speckled with green and red flares that momentarily lit up the balconies and stairways of its forbidding presence. All around, the desert floor was swarming with activity. Giant scorpions crouched in their hundreds, still and silent, waiting for the command that would ignite them into action. Groups of Dreden worked over fiery braziers and anvils, hammering metal into wicked-shaped weapons, but it was the tall, wheeled towers and the corkscrew-like shapes that they contained within their structures that gave a sense of foreboding and destruction.

Amidst all of this activity, a figure appeared, flanked by large lizard-like creatures. He strode forward with a purpose, looking around him and nodding in approval. Abruptly, he stopped as if suddenly aware that he was being watched; his face turned and all those watching saw the piercing, black soulless eyes of Lord Maelstrom staring directly at them.

Cassaria immediately brought her bangles together and with a burst of sparks, the image imploded and disappeared.

'Prince Ameer has always taken council with the Elders, but the time has come for him to lead his people without question, without debate. You have seen the threat to Aridian; you have seen the evil that is Lord Maelstrom and he has sensed your presence.'

One of the Elders stepped forwards. 'How do we know that we can trust the Dreden that say they will join us?'

'You don't know,' said Ameer. 'You also have no idea if this boy,' he indicated to Frog, 'who has faced Lord Maelstrom before, will want to do so again. If he does, you don't know whether he will survive, because when all is said and done, if he fails, we all fail. Aridian will fall and so shall every Dimension.'

The Elders turned in hushed discussion as the others stood, waiting. Frog felt Nadiah's hand gently clasp his and he gave a cautious glance sideways at her, but her gaze was fixed forwards at the group of Elders and so he gave her hand a soft squeeze in return and allowed a pleasant feeling to run through his mind.

After a short while, the sound of conversation stopped and the same Elder stepped forwards again.

'We have always trusted the judgement of the Guardians and we respect the right of Prince Ameer to lead his people. If, as you say, this young boy is prepared to face mortal danger and that those we once mistrusted wish to fight for our survival, then we are truly humbled. As one, we pledge unity and loyalty to Prince Ameer.'

Each and every Elder knelt and bowed their head towards Ameer, but Frog noticed two hesitant figures at the back of the group. The men exchanged a look of acknowledgement and then silently slipped away. Frog had seen that look before and he sensed betrayal.

17

Betrayal

Out in the desert Baron moved stealthily forwards. He needed to get word of Billy's desperate situation to Ameer. He knew that the boy was in grave danger and regretted leaving him in the hands of Belzeera, but he felt that he had done so with no choice. If he had attempted to fight her then both he and Billy would be dead by now, he was sure of that and so, he had made the decision to escape while he could.

He had left the scorpion as soon as he felt that he was a safe distance from Belzeera's stronghold. The creature had hissed at him angrily as he leapt from it and trudged up and over a large ridge of sand. He thought for a moment that it would follow him, even try to kill him, but in the end, he was left to make his journey alone.

That had been what he felt was hours ago. He was sure that he had been heading in the right direction, only a few others equalled his knowledge of the landscape and he knew that he was close to an Aridian crystal farm. What concerned him was whether he could make them believe that he and a select group of Dreden were secretly working with Ameer to forge a united Aridian people.

He reached the edge of a dune and below, there was the Aridian camp nestled in the shelter of a rock formation. To one side, three large Sandspiders crouched as still as statues, the first light of dawn picking out the dark brown hairs on their bodies. Standing close by was a sentry; she was dressed in the robes of the Sisterhood and Baron knew that there would be at least a dozen or so others inside of the tented canopy.

He decided that he had no choice. Honesty was the best policy and he just hoped that they would listen to him. Slowly, he made his way down the sand dune towards her. He was about 20 metres away when she suddenly turned and looked at him. He obeyed his instinct to stop and raise his hands in surrender, but to his surprise, she lifted her arms, making the fists that he knew would generate her extraordinary powers.

He stood helpless as he saw the energy ripple out towards him and with it a force that, more often than not, could stop a man's heart. He could not believe that a member of the Sisterhood would now kill a defenceless Dreden, with no word of warning, no caution.

Two things happened at once. The shock wave hit him off balance along with the searing pain of something sharp embedding itself in his back. The impact spun him around and he looked up to the top of the dune and saw the figure of Zebran, who dropped a crossbow at his feet and clutched his chest when the full effect of the force hit him. Baron witnessed the final moments of the man's wicked and cruel life before

160

his own senses clouded over and he collapsed face down into the sand as the girl rushed to his aid.

Below ground, the Council of Elders had ended and most of them had made their way back to their communities to ready the people for the part that they would have to play in the coming defence of their world.

Frog, The One, Nadiah, Cassaria, Ameer, Fray, Pasha, Jenna and Katar, along with two of the Sisterhood and two of the Elders, all stood in conversation.

'We must ready all of the Sandspiders and their riders,' said Ameer. 'I would suggest that they assemble at Pelmore where we will also need to assess which of the younger spiders and their riders are ready for battle. Katar, will you organise what is needed?'

'Certainly, my Lord Prince. I will also need to consult with Arac-Khan and to make certain of her safety.'

'Whatever you deem is necessary,' said Ameer. 'But you must ensure that an army is assembled and ready for battle.' He turned to the Sisterhood.

'Ladies, I know that you have already been tested and have suffered casualties, but we are in need of the Sisterhood in this encounter, whether it be a last line of defence in our cities and communities or facing the evil on the battlefront.'

The tallest of the women spoke.

'We will be wherever we are needed. Our less experienced students can stay with the communities to fight should the time come, whilst those who have achieved the full powers of Sisterhood will take their place in direct combat.'

'Elders, gather your people,' instructed Cassaria.

'Put those who are vulnerable under the protection of the Sisterhood and send every Aridian who is able to fight to join the ranks of Prince Ameer.'

'And what is our part in this?' asked The One indicating to himself, Frog and Nadiah.

'Your place will be next to me at the time of confrontation with Lord Maelstrom,' said Cassaria. 'What he thinks to be his ultimate strength is, in fact, where his weakness lies. Frog is that weakness; without him, we cannot overcome Lord Maelstrom; without him, Lord Maelstrom cannot achieve his ultimate and final power.

'However, the Slipstream works in mysterious ways. The arrival of The One was not foreseen and the Guardians fear that his presence has added another opportunity to Lord Maelstrom – the blood of the son comes from the father.'

'You mean that a drop of my blood will release the power of the Rune Stone as much as Frog's?' asked The One.

'We are not sure how potent that action would be,' continued Cassaria. 'Or if it would have any effect at all. That is another reason why you and Frog must now remain together at all times. If you are separated then Lord Maelstrom will have two targets, two possible ways to achieve his needs.'

'Was everyone who was here supposed to be trustworthy?' asked Frog.

'Why do you ask?' questioned Ameer.

'Because I think that there are at least two people amongst you who are already sending information to him. I saw them standing at the back earlier on and they disappeared very quickly without talking to anyone else.'

'What did they look like?' asked one of the Elders.

'I don't think that they would pass as twins, but they did look very much alike.'

'I know who you talk of,' confirmed one of the Elders. 'They are two brothers who have become more withdrawn from the Elder Council of late, keeping their views to themselves. There have been concerns about their motives.'

Ameer turned to Jenna. 'Will you seek out the truth for us?'

'With respect to the Elders,' said Jenna, 'we will seek out the truth from all of the Elder Council. If there is betrayal amongst them then we need to be prepared,' she turned to Pasha and Fray. 'Let us seek out the lies and betrayal that could endanger us all.'

A haze surrounded their forms and with a gentle effect, they transformed into the enchanting Firefox. After briefly nuzzling each other, all three scampered across the chamber and out of the far exit.

'It is time for us to take our different paths,' said Cassaria. 'No doubt, if good fortune is with us, then we shall all meet again on the battlefield and put an end to the plague that infests Aridian.'

As Ameer and Katar, the Sisterhood and the Elders left through shadowed archways, Cassaria turned to the others.

'Nadiah will be your guide. She alone amongst you knows the paths and ways of Aridian, above and below its surface. You are to first go to Pelmore and await my calling.'

'But what about Billy?' asked Frog. 'What's happening to him?'

'Billy has someone to watch over him. If all goes well and he plays his part as planned, you will see him soon.'

'And what if it doesn't go well?'

'Do not seal your friend's fate. He is here for a reason. He is not here by accident. There is the design of ancient Magic at work here, the same design that brought us The One and the same Magic that first pulled you into the Slipstream to travel the Dimensions. Focus on what you can do, not what you cannot. Now, you must leave. No more words.'

As Cassaria watched, Nadiah led Frog and The One out of the same archway through which they had entered the chamber and she took them along a narrow winding passageway until it opened out onto another rock platform and a wooden lift cage.

'Do we really have to?' said Frog remembering his precarious journey down to Sanctuary.

'I told you that they're quite safe,' said Nadiah. 'It is a short journey upward. Then we will take a watercourse down through the galleries to Pelmore. We need to go up, to go down.'

'And that's supposed to make me feel better?' Frog replied.

'What's all the fuss? It's just a lift, isn't it?' said The One.

'Just tell me when we get there,' said Frog stepping in, grabbing a handrail and closing his eyes.

Nadiah pulled a lever and the cage slowly bumped its way up into the shaft. Small crystals set into the rock at regular intervals gave them light as they ascended.

'What's at Pelmore?' asked The One.

'The Sandspider hatcheries. It is also the most fortified and deepest place on Aridian,' replied Nadiah.

She looked at Frog. 'Are you scared?'

'Well, this isn't exactly my idea of fun,' he replied.

'No, I mean are you scared about fighting Lord Maelstrom? Because if you are, you don't seem to show it.'

'I'm scared all right. Fighting him the last time was bad enough, but now he's going to be meaner than ever after what I did to him. I can't afford to show that I'm scared. I have to concentrate on doing what's needed, which, by the way, half the time I don't know what it is until it happens. Anyhow, as I see it, I've got an advantage this time.'

'What's that?' asked The One.

'I have my Da –' he stopped himself. 'I have you with me.'

'I don't know how that's going to help you,' said The One. 'I haven't got a clue what I'm supposed to do. Besides, I'm more worried about something really bad happening to you.'

'You mean like getting killed?'

'Killed, hurt, injured,' said The One. 'Does death travel across the Dimensions?'

'Injuries certainly do,' said Frog holding up his hand with the shortened little finger on it. 'I don't think just because you can't see it in our world that it doesn't exist. So, I guess if you die here then you go back dead.'

The lift bumped again, this time with enough force

to make them all grab the handrail. Then it came to a halt.

'What's going on?' asked Frog.

'I don't know,' replied Nadiah craning her neck to look up the lift shaft.

The lift cage gave another shudder and then it jerked upwards with a sudden increase in speed. The crystal lights blurred past them as the cage bounced against the shaft.

'Something's wrong,' shouted Nadiah.

'No kidding,' muttered Frog.

'Whoever is operating the winch has lost control,' she said.

'Either that,' said The One. 'Or someone is in a hurry to meet us.'

'Lay down on the floor,' said Nadiah.

Frog didn't need telling again and The One followed, but not before Frog had drawn his sword and passed his bullwhip to him.

'Here, take this. It's not much, but with a good flick it can cause quite a bit of damage to exposed flesh.'

The One stared into Frog's eyes with a mixture of horror and wonder.

Frog looked back. 'I've had to learn all sorts of things to survive in the Dimensions that I wouldn't even dream of doing back home. Just remember that, inside, I'm still the same person. Trust me.'

The One nodded and took the bullwhip.

Frog could see Nadiah's face strobing in the passing lights. He watched as she braced her body against the shuddering cage, her fists tight and glowing with energy.

'When I say jump, then jump,' she shouted. 'Be prepared to defend yourselves.' No sooner had the words left her mouth than the cage jerked out into open space. 'Jump!'

All three of them tumbled out onto the hard, stone floor. Frog barrel-rolled to one side, narrowly avoiding The One as both of them gained their footing and stood up. Nadiah sprung between them, arms outstretched, her hands shimmering. The lift cage smashed into the ceiling behind them, disintegrating with a splintering crash.

As their eyes focussed in the steady light, they could see that there were at least twelve dark, robed shapes around them, crossbows at the ready.

'Dreden,' shouted Nadiah as she released her power. The shock waves rippled out, knocking figures off their feet and back against the walls, but not before half a dozen arrows let fly. Two hit Nadiah's force and bounced away; the other four speared towards Frog and The One. Without any hesitation, Frog leapt at The One, using his own body as a shield. One of the arrows clanked off the blade of his sword, but the other three hit him square in his chest, their sharp force punching the air out of him. He hit the unforgiving floor and pain exploded across his body, too much for his senses to bear, and the inevitable shroud of blackness draped itself over him as his breath left his lungs.

18

Firefox

All three Firefox had made their separate ways into the tunnels in order to search out the Aridian Council. News of their return spread quickly and most people greeted them with wonder and affection. Young children fearlessly approached them, their small fingers running through the Firefox's soft coats as they passed by. There were a few though, mostly of the older population, who looked on with mistrust and suspicion and gave the Firefox a wide berth.

The majority of the Aridian Council openly approached them, allowing the Firefox to stare deep into their eyes, proving to them that they were loyal Aridians. There were some, however, who did not want to be tested. They hid away, mainly through fear and uncertainty, but amongst them were those that had darker motives.

Fray found himself in a small courtyard. At the centre of it was a circle of six decorated, stone columns, which supported small crystals. He had followed the scent of one particular individual who had left a negative trace in the air. As he approached one of the surrounding doorways, a figure slipped from the shadows and hid behind a stone column. The movement did not go unnoticed to the Firefox's sensitive ears. Aware of danger, Fray morphed into his human form.

'I mean you no harm,' he said to the unseen individual. 'I only seek the truth of your intentions.'

The figure darted to hide behind another column and Fray shifted his position.

'If you have been influenced and confused by the evil powers that seek to destroy us all, then let me help you. I am unarmed. Step out so that I can see you.'

The effect of Fray's soft voice brought the stranger out into the crystal light. He was a middle-aged man dressed in the robes of the Aridian Council, his silver-grey hair resting on his shoulders.

'You carry the Guardian Cassaria's Magic with you. She is an imposter,' he said, echoing Belzeera's words.

'No,' said Fray. 'You have been bewitched by lies and false promises. Let me help you to see the truth.'

Fray held out his hand in friendship. A smile crossed the man's face and he, too, held his hand out and stepped forward. Fray saw the glint of steel as the man's other hand came out from the folds of his robe and his expression darkened. His lips stretched across his teeth and his face contorted with rage.

'You lie!' he screamed and he lunged at Fray's throat with a short-bladed dagger.

Fray grasped the man's wrist; it took both hands and all of his strength to push the sharp steel to one side. The man twisted himself around, grabbing at Fray's cloak with his other hand, intent on getting behind him. Fray could see the danger and dropped to his knees, forcing his assailant to topple over him. He felt a sharp tug on his cloak as the man hung on, dragging him forward to fall sideways onto the stone floor. Before he could recover, the man was up and on top of him, straddling his body.

Fray reached up, grasping at the man's wrist once again. He could feel his arms weakening as the man pushed the blade closer and closer to his throat. He could see the reflection of Belzeera's image in the man's eyes and all of the wickedness and despair spilled out and into his senses. He knew that even if he now morphed into a Firefox, he would be killed. The man's grip was too powerful. His strength was unnatural.

From the corner of his eye, Fray suddenly saw a blur of red fur leaping through the air. However, the first that the man knew of another presence was when sharp teeth clasped around his wrist and bit deep enough to sever the tendons. The knife clattered to the floor as the man lurched back in surprise and pain. Fray kicked at his legs, taking them out from under him. As he collapsed onto the ground, the Firefox released his arm and leapt to one side where, in an instant, it morphed into the familiar figure of Pasha. They stood over the man and watched as he scrambled back from them, clutching his bloody wrist.

'Are you all right?' Pasha asked Fray.

'I'll survive, thanks to you,' he said, rubbing the red marks that had already formed on his neck from the man's chokehold.

'None of you will survive. She will destroy you all,' said the man's deep voice as he managed to get close to the knife again and grab it.

'No!' shouted Fray.

'You'll not get her secrets from me,' he yelled and there was nothing that either of them could do. He plunged the blade into his own chest, ending his life in front of them.

'What sort of evil is it that forces these poor souls to sacrifice their own lives?' asked Fray.

'The same happened to another that I pursued,' replied Pasha. 'Only when I confronted him, he chose to leap from a high balcony to his doom.'

'There are those that will blame us for these deaths,' said Fray.

'And there are many that will know the truth,' said Pasha. 'We have waited too long to come out of exile to return to the community. Let us do what good we can to help fight the dark menace that would enslave us all.' She gave Fray a comforting hug. 'Now, let us search for Jenna and account for all members of the council, good or bad.'

Together, they changed shape back into their Firefox forms and made their way back out into the corridors and alleyways.

Elsewhere, Jenna had reached a small square and paused to allow some young children to pet and stroke her while she gathered her thoughts. She took the time to focus on sensing out the identity of the person that she had been trailing.

The group surrounding her soon expanded so that she was encircled by children, parents and other curious adults, and she could feel the warmth of acceptance rising through her in a way that had been denied to her kind for so long. Basking in the adulation, however, had left her exposed and she was unable to sense danger until large hands grabbed the scruff of fur around her neck and hoisted her out of the crowd. Another pair of hands grasped her hind legs and tail.

'This is an abomination and a threat to us all,' shouted the man whose fingers dug into the skin of her neck.

'These creatures are full of deceit and will divide us all as they did in the past,' preached the woman who was also holding on to her.

Jenna knew that her only hope was to change into her human form. Her transformation drew gasps from the crowd, and her sudden size and weight took her two assailants by surprise, both of them losing their grips. As Jenna dropped to the floor, the man, however, was quick to react and he fell upon her, pinning her to the ground.

'See how she uses her trickery and magic,' he shouted. 'She is part of the evil that has come to Aridian and threatens us.'

The woman scrabbled to hold down Jenna's legs.

'No! No!' pleaded Jenna. 'We only mean to help.'

'Silence,' shouted the man and he drew back his arm, ready to strike her across the head.

Jenna closed her eyes, anticipating the pain, but none came. She slowly opened one eye and was over-joyed to see Fray standing over her, his brown hand closed around the man's fist.

'Let our sister go,' he commanded.

She then felt the pressure relieved from her legs as Pasha pulled the woman away.

Fray looked deep into the man's eyes, drawing on the truth. 'There is no more evil in us than there is in you,' he said at last. 'All that you have in your mind is fear and confusion. You are weak when you need to be strong.'

Pasha had looked into the mind of the woman.

'This woman is the same,' she said. 'Her mind has not been infected by the evil from the surface.'

'Both of you go in peace,' said Fray. 'It is not a sin to be afraid, but do not pass that fear on to others.'

The man looked at Fray and Pasha. Then down at Jenna.

'I am so sorry,' he said blinking back tears. He took the woman's hand and with downcast heads, they pushed their way out through the crowd.

Fray helped Jenna to her feet. 'Are you all right?' he asked.

'My neck hurts,' she replied, rubbing it gently. 'But it could have been worse.'

A small child moved forward and took Jenna's hand.

'Are you going to chase the bad people away?' she asked.

'I hope so,' said Jenna. 'I really hope so.'

19

Pursued

The One's face was pale and ashen as he turned Frog's limp body over. Three dark, shafted arrows were embedded in his robes. He cradled Frog in his arms, pulling him close to his chest.

'My son,' he sobbed. 'My son.'

Nadiah backed towards him, her arms still outstretched at the fallen Dreden.

'Carry him. Quickly, we must go,' she ordered.

The One looked up. 'What's the point? He's dead. My son is dead.'

'If he is dead then there is little hope for any of us,' said Nadiah. 'But while there is still Cassaria and the ancient Magic of the Guardians then there is still hope for him. Now pick up his sword, carry him and follow me.'

The One gently hoisted Frog's body up and quickly followed Nadiah through a small exit, then down a narrow passageway. As they moved on, they could hear the gathering voices and urgent shouts of more Dreden coming from behind them.

Nadiah stopped. 'Wait,' she ordered and studied the rough rock face on one side of the passage.

The Dreden voices became louder, closer.

'What are you doing?' asked The One. 'They're nearly on us.'

'Just wait.' She ran her hands across the surface of the rock, the ink black shadows permanently fixed in places by the steady crystal light. 'Yes, here it is,' she said and slid her hand into a dark space then slowly withdrew it. There was a grating noise as the rock wall gave a shudder and moved to one side in the shape of a coarse doorway.

'Get in,' she ordered.

The One stepped into what was a small room lit by two crystals. There was a camp-style bed to one side and a small table displaying various jugs and bowls. As he laid Frog's body onto the bed, he heard the doorway close behind him and then Nadiah was there at his side.

'Let me see,' she said. 'Bring that crystal closer. Hold it above him.'

The One did as he was told while Nadiah tenderly removed Frog's headdress. She moved his face from side to side; his skin was now pale and his lips tinged with blue. To The One's surprise, she leant over and placed her mouth over Frog's.

'He still breathes,' she announced. 'But only just. Help me loosen his robes.'

As gently and as quickly as they could, they parted the layers of Frog's robes and as they did so, they found that the arrows moved away with the material.

'What's happened?' asked The One.

'Look,' said Nadiah. 'No blood.'

Both stared in amazement as they moved apart the

last layer of material to reveal a strange-looking, vest-type undergarment.

'What is it?' asked Nadiah.

'Whatever it is, it saved his life, but it's also killing him. He can't breathe; it's become too tight.'

After wrestling with the robes, they managed to untie the garment and remove it, but Frog's breathing did not improve. His chest already bore three close-set purple bruises and the colour of his lips had become darker.

This time it was The One who leant over and put his lips to Frog's mouth, blowing breath into his lungs, administering the kiss of life. Nadiah watched tensely as Frog's chest rose and fell with the rhythm of The One's breath entering his body until, finally and with relief, Frog's eyes opened and he pushed himself up, gasping air in and out of his lungs. A cold sweat appeared on his brow as his breathing gradually eased and reclaimed its natural rhythm.

Nadiah fetched some water in a small bowl and Frog drank gratefully.

'I thought that I'd lost you there,' said The One.

'I put a lot of faith in an old friend's gift,' said Frog, rubbing his chest.

'You need to thank him when you get the chance,' said Nadiah inspecting the Dragon-skin waistcoat.

'Unfortunately, he lost his life on Castellion,' said Frog, fondly remembering Sir Dragonslayer.

'I'm sure that he would have been proud of you,' said The One. 'As I am.' He squeezed Frog's hand affectionately. 'Now, how are you feeling? Can you stand?'

Frog slowly got to his feet, still rubbing his chest.

'Actually, I'm okay apart from feeling like I've been hit by a black belt at Taekwondo.' He glanced around. 'Where are we?'

Nadiah passed some water to The One and moved to the outline of the closed door, pressing her ear against the wall.

'In one of the many shelters that are built into the tunnel network,' she answered. 'There are Dreden searching for us. We have been betrayed.'

'So, what do we do now?' asked Frog.

'We get ready for the run of our lives. We must take the waterways to Pelmore.' She made her way to a wooden door at the back of the room. 'We need to leave. Can you continue?'

'Sure,' Frog replied as he struggled with his robes. It was obvious that he was in pain.

'Here, let me help,' said The One.

Ten minutes later, with Frog dressed, they were steadily making their way along a very narrow corridor that had led out from the back of the room. Long shadows stretched behind them from the small crystal that Nadiah now carried as she guided the way.

It wasn't long before they heard the familiar sound of rushing water ahead of them and a brighter light shone from around a bend. Nadiah signalled for them to crouch down as they approached the tunnel's exit, not knowing if more Dreden would be waiting for them. She passed the crystal back to The One before she clenched her fists and leapt out into the open.

For a moment, she was lost to view and the others froze, bracing themselves against any following onslaught. Finally, she called to them.

'Hurry, we need to get to the flumes. I can hear shouting in the tunnels.'

They followed her across the opening to a row of flumes, bobbing gently up and down in a gully. Nadiah ran to a row of three wooden levers protruding out of a wall and pulled them all downwards. She then quickly jumped into the first flume and Frog and The One followed her lead by jumping into the second. She pulled another lever and both flumes were pushed into the waiting tunnel by the force of the water, which suddenly seemed to flow with more urgency.

'Are we supposed to be moving this fast?' shouted Frog as he held onto the sides.

'I've opened up the sluice gates to let more water into the system. We need to get away as fast as we can,' she shouted back. 'Hold on. This is going to be a rough ride.'

They shot out of the short tunnel at breakneck speed, the watercourse now carrying them along a gully suspended across an enormous cavern. Frog looked over the side and wished that he hadn't; a network of waterways criss-crossed below them for hundreds of feet before fading into a grey mist.

'Where's the bottom?' he pleaded to The One as he increased his grip so tightly that his knuckles turned white, but his voice could not be heard over the raging water.

They powered into another tunnel, a steep curve in the semi darkness taking them by surprise, before they once again emerged amongst the suspended watercourses.

'Are you all right?' The One asked Frog.

'I've felt better. Still, at least it's taken my mind off of the pain in my chest.'

Nadiah turned to speak, but was distracted by something above them.

'Duck!' she shouted.

Frog turned to follow her gaze as an arrow whizzed past his ear.

'Blimey! That was close,' he gasped as he was pulled down into the flume by The One.

'You're going to push your luck, my boy. Weren't three arrows in the chest enough for you?'

Two more arrows thudded into the side of the flume.

'Obviously not,' Frog grumbled.

Nadiah looked across at them huddled together and shouted, 'You're too far away. I can't shield you and I daren't project my force at them in case I bring down the cables that are holding up our watercourse.'

Frog took a second glance. About 30 metres above them and following the same watercourse, ten Dreden occupied four more flumes. Thankfully, the unsteady movement as they travelled was making it hard for them to aim with any accuracy. As Frog watched, one of the Dreden stood up and braced a foot against the side of his flume, raising his crossbow and putting The One in his sights.

The flume juddered against the trough, tilted back and threw the reckless Dreden over its side. Frog saw the sheer horror in the man's eyes as he fell past him, his arms waving and clawing at the air in desperation as he plummeted, screaming into the waiting mist below.

The distance between their flumes was increasing as

Nadiah disappeared into a tunnel ahead of them. By the time Frog and The One entered, she was out of her flume and standing on another small platform.

There was a junction in the waterway and she pulled a lever, which opened a gate sending Frog and The One in another direction.

'I'll hold them up for a while and then join you on the lower levels,' she called as she closed the gate after them.

Their flume jerked left and into a new tunnel. A few moments of darkness and they were out again, this time high up in the roof of another cavern, crossing a different network of watercourses.

'She's crazy. We should have faced them together,' complained Frog.

'She knows what she's doing. Trust her,' said The One.

The flume sped on across the cavern, into another tunnel and turned sharply into the brief darkness and back out amongst more suspended waterways.

Suddenly, there was a dull thump as a fist-sized rock landed in the flume between them. Frog frowned at the object as The One picked it up. A larger chunk then sailed past them and looking up, they could see the centre of the cavern's roof disintegrating high above them.

'What now?' asked Frog.

'When you make enemies you don't do it by halves, do you?' replied The One.

As they watched pieces of the roof fall around them, an enormous grey lizard, looking like a gigantic Komodo dragon, clawed its way through the jagged opening. Its soulless eyes turned towards them as a forked, blood-red tongue flicked in and out of its lipless mouth. With astounding agility, it crawled across the roof of the cavern, its body suspended by the same natural ability as a gecko. It reached out a clawed limb and dislodged another chunk of rock, which crashed down onto the waterway behind them, smashing a section into splinters so that water cascaded out into space and no longer fed their channel, which now rocked wildly.

As the water drained away, their flume came to a halt, trapped halfway across the cavern. The reptile continued to claw away at the ceiling sending more debris smashing down; this time the waterway in front of them disintegrated into fragments. Their flume now hung in a short section of channel suspended only by four cables anchored far above them in the ceiling. It swayed dangerously.

'It's heading for the cables,' said The One. 'We've got to get off this thing.'

Frog looked down. The nearest waterway was at least 20 metres below them.

'I appear to have left my wings at home, so unless you've brought yours then flying is out of the question.'

The One grimaced a smile. 'Now is not the time for sarcasm.' He gripped the cable nearest to him. 'Grab the other, quickly,' he ordered.

The other end of the watercourse dipped wildly and the flume slid away as two of its supporting cables snaked downwards, torn out of their anchor points by the monster above. Frog and The One hung suspended

181

by the remaining two cables, their feet scrabbling for purchase on the broken section of the watercourse.

'We've got to get to that water chute below,' said The One. 'Climb on my back. I've got an idea.'

He slid the bullwhip from his shoulder, the long leather lash uncoiled out from his hand like a dark snake. Frog was gripping him piggyback-style as The One flicked the whip out towards another of the network of cables. Frog guessed his intentions.

'You've got to be kidding!' he shouted.

The third of the cables slackened and fell past, sending them spinning wildly, suspended by the last support. Frog looked up to see a large claw about to scythe into their final lifeline.

'Do it! Do it now!' he roared at The One.

In a way, the slight drop that followed did them a favour. The whip cracked out like a tentacle, wrapping itself around one of the other suspension cables as they fell. The momentum of the fall swung them like a pendulum out and across the waterway. After two passes, The One managed to grab the cable.

They hung there; The One's breathing fast and harsh; Frog's heart thumped in his chest.

'When I release the whip, we jump. It's our only chance. After three.'

Frog nodded in agreement.

'One, two ...' he flicked the whip and they fell the 3 metres into the flowing waters of another trough.

'What happened to three?' asked Frog as they both landed awkwardly in the chute.

'Three would have been too late. Look, it's heading for the cables again.'

Above them, the lizard was in frenzy, lashing out at cables, trying to bring down the whole network of waterways.

As they were propelled ever faster along the chute, their clothes became heavy and sodden with the water. The dark mouth of a tunnel loomed in front of them. Water foamed and bubbled as it sucked them in and they were swept into the gloom and an unseen fate.

20

An Unexpected Guest

Nadiah lay low in the flume, waiting for the Dreden to enter the chamber, listening to their shouts.

They make more noise than a herd of Saurs at mealtime, she thought.

At least a dozen Dreden crashed out of the tunnel, swords and crossbows at the ready. They stopped, surveying the chamber, their eyes searching for their prey.

'There,' whispered one of them and he pointed to the pale, blue light emanating from a flume.

'What is it?' asked another.

'Sisterhood, if I'm not mistaken. Hiding and ready to strike,' quietly announced the group's leader.

Eight crossbows and four vicious-looking spears were immediately trained on the flume.

'Come out and keep your hands behind your back,' the leader ordered.

There was no reply, no movement. Nadiah kept still.

The group of Dreden shuffled forward forming a semi-circle, slowly edging themselves closer to the flume, 3 metres, 2 metres.

'Show yourself now or die where you lay,' he barked as nervous spittle sprayed out of his mouth.

Still there was no movement. Nadiah remained motionless and ready to strike.

'Then die!' he screamed and there could be no escape as they lunged forwards together, arrows flying into the flume, spear tips thrust at the unseen figure. When their assault reached its climax, the group came to an unsteady halt on the platform's edge. One of them jumped into the flume and for a moment, he stood, puzzled, staring at the solitary, glowing rock crystal.

'Looking for someone?' said Nadiah as she rose up from another flume at the far end of the platform. Before they could respond, her robes parted to reveal two electric-blue fists. She turned them, palms out, and the devastating power undulated forwards, the soundless pressure hitting the group of men, tossing them against the cave walls and crushing the life out of them in an instant.

Further voices echoed from the waterway's entrance; it was more of the pursuing Dreden in their flumes. She lifted one hand and directed a pulse of energy at the small tunnel, which shook and trembled as the roof caved in, blocking the entrance and denying the Dreden further passage. She pulled a lever and without looking back, allowed the flume to carry her out in search of her lost companions.

Through tunnels and across caverns, pushing levers and switching waterways, she travelled ever downward, ever closer to Pelmore, praying that Frog and The One had found their way to safety.

It took her over half an hour to reach the end of her journey and her flume finally emerged from a tunnel and into a larger cave. At the far end, a waterwheel with oblong buckets connected together by lengths of cable, each large enough to carry individual flumes, rotated out of the ceiling and into a pool. Each bucket disappeared below the surface before rising up full of water and journeying aloft to recycle the water, and any flumes that were collected, back into the system.

Four Aridians stood guard; the emblem of a white spider adorned their black robes. They moved towards her as her flume jostled itself into the narrow causeway that ran alongside the platform.

'A small boy, roughly my age, and a tall man with a scar on his forehead; have they come this way?' she asked hurriedly.

'None has come out of that tunnel except for you, Sisterhood,' said one of the guards. 'Dreden and giant lizards are reported in the upper levels and some of the waterways have been destroyed. All upper gates into Pelmore have been closed since sundown when orders were given to stop the water flow.'

As if to affirm the truth of what he had said, the mechanism of scoops and cables slowly juddered to a halt.

'These that you seek; are they Dreden?' asked the guard.

'No. They are our friends and may be our salvation. I need to get to Prince Ameer, quickly,' she answered and clambered out of the flume.

'Escort the Sisterhood to the Prince,' he ordered one of the others. 'If they should get here after you have gone, then I will personally deliver them into safe keeping,' he added to Nadiah. 'However, if they are behind you, then they really are in trouble. Very soon, the watercourses will drain and they will be stranded in the system.'

As Nadiah and her escort travelled through Pelmore's underground walkways and avenues, she could see the anxious faces of Aridians everywhere. There was no panic, but a sense of controlled urgency and uncertainty filled the air. Above all, she noticed that the majority of the people who were to-ing and fro-ing were either young children or the elderly. All who were fit and able-bodied had gone to play their part in Aridian's defence against Lord Maelstrom.

They turned a corner into a small, open plaza. Intricate carvings adorned the balconies on either side, which jutted out as though defying gravity. Rows of arches, almost Moroccan in style, followed along the balconies above and below, and the stone beneath their feet was worn smooth by generations of Aridians.

Ahead of them stood two more guards dressed in black robes, their hands resting on the dark handles of long, curved swords suspended from their waistbands.

After just a few steps across the plaza, Nadiah's escort stopped and turned to her.

'I must return to my duties. We will keep watch for your friends and if there is any news, I will send a messenger.' He touched his forehead and chest in salute and then made his way back across the square.

Nadiah approached the two guards.

'You have been expected, Sisterhood,' said one. 'Through the archway, turn left and along the passage,' he instructed.

Nadiah followed the directions until at the end of the

passage, there were two more guards, again wearing the black robes with the white spider insignia of Pelmore.

Without a word, they pushed open the double doors behind them and allowed Nadiah to step into a brightly lit room. The doors closed silently behind her.

Her eyes accustomed themselves to the light and she made out two, seated figures, wrapped in thick towelling with cups of hot brew in their hands. Ameer stood beside them and a smile crossed his face as he greeted Nadiah.

'They were found, floundering in one of the reservoirs, luckily by two of the Sisterhood who were checking the area.'

Frog beamed with delight at the sight of Nadiah.

'Are you all right? We thought that we'd lost you to the Dreden.' He stood to move towards her, but quickly sat back down as the towel slipped and threatened to cause him embarrassment.

'I'm fine,' she smiled. 'Although, there are now a few less Dreden to fight alongside Lord Maelstrom. What happened to you two?'

Frog and The One relayed the events of their journey to Nadiah, ending with their surprise fall from a feeder chute that carried water to one of the underground reservoirs. They had exited about 3 metres high up and out into thin air before splashing gracelessly down into the water. Their sodden robes threatened to pull them down, but thankfully they managed to struggle free of them before being helped to safety by the two girls who, after listening to their story, brought them straight to Ameer.

The doors opened and a guard entered carrying two bundles of clean robes.

'Use that room over there to change,' said Ameer, indicating a panelled door.

Frog and The One gratefully took the garments and left to change while Nadiah and Ameer exchanged information.

'I understand that the upper gates have been closed,' said Nadiah.

'Yes,' confirmed Ameer. 'Any Dreden in the tunnels and waterways will be trapped there. We've posted groups of guards to ensure that they do not enter the city itself. As for the creature that Frog and The One encountered, there have been no other reports or sightings of it and it is hoped that it has returned to the surface having been unable to pursue them. I think that we can safely assume that it is of Belzeera's making and we can expect other such monstrosities amongst Lord Maelstrom's minions.'

Frog re-entered the room closely followed by The One. Their new white robes now carried the black spider symbol of Aridian. At the same moment, a guard entered from the corridor and approached Ameer.

'My Lord Prince, the Sisterhood have brought a prisoner from the surface who insists on speaking with you. We would not bother you in other circumstances, but he was carrying this.' He held out a small piece of brown parchment; the spider insignia of Pelmore was etched upon it.

Ameer's forehead creased and his face filled with unease.

'Is he here?'

'Yes, my Lord.'

'Then, bring him in. I hope that you have been gentle with him for he is a good friend and ally.'

This time the guard's face showed concern.

'He has been injured, my Lord, but that was not of our doing.'

He opened the door and another guard entered, his arm around Baron's waist, helping to support him. Baron had his arm in a sling and dried blood stained the front of his robes.

Frog could not help staring. This was the closest that he had been to a Dreden and he was curiously drawn to the man's angular face. The thick, shiny skin of his cheeks and forehead and the sharp ridge of his nose made his features look as though they had been put together in sections. He had a strong, square jaw line and long, lank black hair, which cascaded down over his shoulders. Frog didn't think that the man looked particularly unfriendly or vicious as he had expected.

Ameer hastily moved to aid his friend, guiding him to a seat and dismissing the guards.

'How badly are you hurt?'

'I'll live,' he grimaced. 'The Sisterhood have tended to me well, but more importantly I bring news of the boy.'

Frog stepped forwards. 'Do you mean Billy? What's happened to Billy?'

Baron studied Frog for a moment. 'I know your image and I hope that you can live up to the bravery of your friend who carries it with such pride.'

'What's happened to him?' Frog insisted.

Baron lowered his eyes. 'He is in the hands of Belzeera. I had to leave him. I am ashamed, but I had

190

no choice. She would have killed us both. I sense that she already knew of Billy's disguise. She has eyes everywhere and assassins ready to do her bidding. I am only grateful that fate has been kind to bring me here.'

'What of the alliance?' asked Ameer. 'Does it still hold?'

'I have recruited many followers, enough for an army, but how many of them will hold true against Lord Maelstrom's influence I am not sure. They are in small groups scattered across Aridian. Their captains are waiting for my word and instructions.'

'When are we going to rescue Billy?' interrupted Frog.

'There will be no rescue,' replied Ameer. 'There was never intended to be one.'

'Well, if you won't go then I will,' argued Frog as he snatched up his sword and turned to the door.

The One put a hand on Frog's shoulder. 'Wait.'

He turned to Ameer. 'You can't be serious. How can you leave a boy in such dangerous circumstances?'

'Billy was sent to mislead Belzeera. If she has discovered his true identity then she will also have learnt a lot more. Cassaria has educated me much about the ways and powers of Belzeera and I would guess that she will use Billy as an instrument of power. He is too valuable for her to destroy, for the time being at least.'

He faced Frog. 'She will use him as a weakness against you, young Frog. She has already provoked a reckless reaction. If you try to rescue him, she will succeed in drawing you into her clutches and to the hands of Lord Maelstrom. Billy carries the Magic of the Guardians with him. Cassaria has given him as much protection as she can. We can only hope that his spirit is strong enough to carry him through his ordeal. You must not fail him by losing faith in him.'

'But he's my best friend,' whispered Frog in a low voice.

Ameer knelt down and put his hands on Frog's shoulders. He looked him straight in the eyes. 'I know that you are worried about your friend, but remember there is also a greater responsibility and challenge that rests with you. You are the only one amongst us who has faced this evil adversary before. You are the legend, the prophecy. You are our hopes and inspiration.

'Know this, my young friend; I will be proud to stand beside you. I would gladly give my life so that you can defeat the menace that threatens us, as would many others that have not even met you. Even this young girl, Nadiah, would pay the ultimate sacrifice to ensure that you fulfil your purpose. I know that this man beside you loves you for who you really are. He is The One, in your world and ours, and he is with you for a reason. You are not alone. Billy is not alone. So, let us prepare for his release and the release of all Aridian.'

Frog took a deep breath, searching for the words. 'It's hard for me. I don't feel thirteen anymore. I don't want to grow up yet. Grown-ups get far too serious. It's fun being a kid. I certainly don't want to die. Nor do I want anyone else to die on my account, but if all of this – the Slipstream, the Dimensions and me being chosen to try and put everything right – is going to make sense, then I'd better get on with it. But please try to remember;

inside, I'm really just a boy who is trying to make the best of what he can do.'

Ameer stood and looked at The One. 'I envy you for who you really are. If I ever have a son and heir, then I can only hope that he has this boy's qualities.'

'Thank you,' acknowledged The One, pride filling his face.

Ameer looked to Nadiah. 'There are resting rooms prepared in the apartments above us. Use them as you will. The servants will provide for you. All you need do is ask. We will meet back here tomorrow evening. Then I will have more news concerning our departure and final destination.'

21

Pelmore

'Before we rest, I would like to show you a little of what we are fighting to save,' said Nadiah and led them back across the plaza. They walked through a high, narrow corridor and then out into a surprisingly bustling area of Pelmore. It was a street market with stalls selling all manner of goods. The smell of rich, aromatic herbs and spices hung in the air along with the ripe, bloody smell of fresh meat. Grey earthenware jugs and bowls were displayed somewhat precariously on one stall while green Atemoya was piled up on another.

'Where does all of this come from?' asked Frog.

'It is all made or grown either here in Pelmore or in the surrounding communities,' said Nadiah.

Frog found it strange how easily he took the light for granted and forgot that they were underground. The crystals that hung on great chandeliers or sat high on stone plinths distributed the light evenly wherever they walked.

'I find it incredible that you can sustain and provide for a whole population underground,' remarked The One.

'When the two suns burnt away life on the surface of Aridian, thankfully our world had something to give us back below its surface,' said Nadiah. 'Let me show you something wonderful.'

She led them to the base of what turned out to be a winding stone staircase and after a long climb, of so many steps that Frog lost count, they emerged onto a large balcony. Meshed ropes formed a waist-high barrier to ensure that no one could topple over the edge. The sound of thundering water assaulted their ears. The view took both Frog's and The One's breath away. They were two-thirds up a colossal cavern and the ceiling above them was concealed by a fine mist, which drifted, fog-like, in clouds across the vast expanse. Carved into the sides of the cavern were rows of terraces, each one growing different forms of vegetation.

An immense and beautiful waterfall cascaded out of the rock face to their left and its flow disappeared into clouds of vapour far below. A rainbow, its colours the most vivid that Frog had ever seen, arched out of the mist. To their right and rising above the vapour were the tops of numerous trees, their big broad leaves palm-like in appearance.

'This is just one of the many resource farms that we have,' shouted Nadiah over the noise of the waterfall.

She could see from the looks on their faces that Frog and The One were too enthralled by the panorama to respond and so she stood back and let them drink in the view for a while. Eventually, she persuaded them to follow her back down the stairway to a seated area by the market where they all sat down. She then disappeared through a door and shortly emerged with a cold drink for each of them.

'Atemoya juice,' she announced.

They sat for a while in silence, sipping at the refreshing liquid and watching Aridians go about their business. Frog observed that much of the attire worn was now of a lighter style, almost ancient Roman or Greek in its fashion. Now and again, a face would glance in their direction, give a half-bow or a nod mainly towards Nadiah and then move on.

'So, what's the plan now?' asked The One, finally breaking their silence.

'We must rest,' said Nadiah. 'It has been many hours since we slept and I am sure that you, like myself, must feel weary,'

It wasn't until that moment that Frog realised how tired he actually felt. The pain in his chest had gone, mainly due to some salve that Ameer had given him to rub in earlier. In fact, the effect of healing had been almost instantaneous and when he had changed into his clean robes, he noticed that the three dark purple bruises had faded away. He did, however, ache everywhere else; the buffeting that he had experienced on the last part of their journey had taken its toll.

The One echoed Frog's thoughts. 'I must admit that I could do with a rest as I do feel a bit tender in places,' he admitted and stretched and massaged a shoulder. 'I should imagine that very soon we're going to need all of the energy that we can raise.'

They finished their drinks then Nadiah led the way back through the main doors, past the guards, along a short passage, up a flight of steps and out onto one of the balconies which overhung the plaza.

'Here are your rooms,' she told them and indicated to the first door that they reached. 'I will be next door. Someone will call us in good time, but should you need anything just ring the bell chord in your room. Sleep well.'

'Thank you, Nadiah,' said The One. 'And thank you for looking after us.'

'Yeah. Thanks,' echoed Frog, smiling kindly.

Before he knew it, Nadiah leant forward and kissed his cheek before opening the door to her room and closing it behind her. Frog stood there with his face the colour of a ripe cherry.

'Come on, Romeo,' said The One, then opened their door and guided a slightly dazed Frog into its softly lit, warm interior.

The beds looked so welcoming that they both lay down without a second thought. Neither of them could remember falling asleep, but they each had differing dreams. The One relived the enjoyment of being with his wife and son on a more peaceful world; visions of happier times when they were together as a family and the warmth of love carried him through his dream.

Frog had drifted into an uneasy vision. He was back home in the kitchen of his house. However, something was wrong; everything was covered in dust. The wooden breakfast table was smashed, broken glass littered the floor and dangerous shards stuck viciously out of the carpet in the hall. He walked nervously and carefully to the foot of the stairs. The house was a mess, completely ransacked. He heard himself calling. 'Mum? Mum?'

He was drawn to his room, the door slightly ajar, beckoned him to push it and on doing so, it swung open slowly at an impossible angle. His eyes fell upon his bed, torn to pieces, and then he froze as the words scratched deeply into the wall above it burned into his mind.

I KNOW WHO YOU ARE AND I AM COMING FOR YOU.

Then, the unmistakable voice of Lord Maelstrom echoed in his head.

'I know who you are and I am coming for you.'

He turned and ran, instinct taking over. He took the stairs, two steps at a time, almost falling. Then, out through the kitchen door, down the path to the orchard where his journey into the Dimensions had begun, he collapsed, sobbing into his own arms, but he could hear his name being called in the distance.

'Frog! Frog! What's wrong? What is it?'

He knew the voice. It was his father's.

'Frog! Frog! Speak to me.'

Then he was awake. The One was sitting beside him with a hand on Frog's sweat-drenched head.

'What's wrong? You were crying in your sleep.'

Frog sat up, gathering his thoughts and looked around the room. 'It was him,' he cried. 'He got inside my head. He's done it before.'

The One handed Frog a cup of water. 'Here, drink this.'

Frog drank gratefully, his senses now coming fully awake.

'Better?'

'Yes thanks.'

'Tell you what,' comforted The One. 'Shuffle over. There must be enough room on this bed for two of us. I'm sure that we've only been asleep for a short while so let's get what rest we can and if he comes back just call out my name. Then he'll have two of us to deal with.'

Frog smiled and, surprisingly, laid back and drifted into a dreamless sleep, as did The One, until they were woken many hours later by Nadiah knocking on their door.

After they had washed and dressed, Nadiah arranged for a selection of cold meats and fruits to be brought to their room, which they ate until not a scrap was left, such were their appetites. When their plates were clean, a guard arrived with a message for them to meet Ameer in the room where their previous meeting had taken place. And so it was that the three of them found themselves seated at a large, oblong table with Ameer, Katar (who had arrived some hours earlier) and Baron, who was now wearing Pelmorian robes decorated with the spider insignia.

'Today is a step forward to our future,' said Ameer. 'Baron may be just one man, but he is the first Dreden to wear the robes of an Aridian for many, many years. I look forward to when all of our people are reunited as one nation again under the symbol of the Sandspider.'

Baron stood. 'I have only the same wish, but before this can be accomplished we must rid our world of Lord Maelstrom and his evil influences that have misled and enslaved my kinsfolk into his service.

Unfortunately, they are divided and I know that the most painful challenge for my followers will be to fight their fellow Dreden. I can only hope that when the time comes, they will rise to that challenge.' He turned to Frog. 'I pledge myself to you and all that you stand for. I am truly sorry for deserting your brave friend, but there was no choice. If I could change places with him, then I gladly would.'

'That's makes two of us,' said Frog.

'Let us focus on saving Billy and defeating our enemies,' announced Ameer as he unrolled a large map across the table. It was quite plain and made up of different hues of brown. Frog thought that the irregular circles that dominated its surface resembled the isobars on a weather map.

'Now, to business,' said Ameer. 'This is where Belzeera's tower is sited and it is here where we will confront Lord Maelstrom's army.' He pointed to an area marked as the Plain of Sighs.

'Why there?' asked Nadiah.

'Because we need to draw all of his resources away from anywhere else that they may be attacking, above and below ground. We do not want to spread the fighting across Aridian. The battle has to be final and conclusive. If we cannot defeat him this way, then we never will. High sand dunes surround the plain except for one place, a narrow gully to the east, which we will hopefully be able to use to our advantage. We will also be able to approach from the elevated positions on either side.'

Katar spoke for the first time. 'Most of the experienced and battle-ready Sandspiders, along with their riders, are making their way to the stable areas closer to the surface to join those that are already there. Tonight, Ameer will join them to organise our advance to the Plain of Sighs. His captains have been briefed and are waiting with all those that can carry a weapon and fight on foot. They are already positioned across the subsurface waiting for the signal to join us.'

'What's our part in this? When are we going to the surface?' asked Nadiah.

'The three of you are to meet up with Cassaria as planned,' replied Katar. 'Later this evening, I am to escort you to a secret location known only to her and myself. There, she will prepare you for whatever part it is that you must play. I am then to join Ameer in command of the Sandspiders.'

'It is time for me to take my leave,' announced Baron. 'I go to find out who is loyal to our cause and gather them around me. They will each be given one of these to wear so that all shall know which Dreden fight the cause for Aridian.' He held up a white headdress with the black Sandspider symbol upon it. 'I shall not see you again until the time of reckoning. May fortune be with us all.' He touched his head and chest in salute. As he walked to the door, Frog could see that Baron was stiff in his movements and that his injury was still troubling him.

'Will he be all right?' he asked.

'He is a warrior,' said Ameer. 'He will survive.'

'Do you know how large his following is?' asked The One.

'Baron estimates that probably only half of the Dreden population have truly fallen under Belzeera's influence, which means that when the time comes, with his army, we should outnumber them six to one,' answered Ameer.

'But they have giant scorpions and lizards,' added Frog.

'And we have Sandspiders, the power of the Sisterhood and the Magic of a Guardian,' replied Ameer.

'All I'm saying,' warned Frog, 'is, don't underestimate Lord Maelstrom.'

'My dear Frog, you've forgotten that we have one more thing on our side,' said Ameer.

'What's that?' he asked.

'You.'

The One leant forwards. 'And you have forgotten a very important fact, Ameer.'

Ameer looked puzzled. 'Which is?'

'You also have me.'

Frog smiled, full of pride for the man that, for now, he could only call The One.

After short goodbyes, they left Ameer studying his map. He had given them all a warm embrace and touched his forehead and chest in salute.

'All that needs to be said has been said,' were his parting words.

22

The Hatcheries

'Have we got time to visit the Hatcheries?' asked Nadiah. 'I think that Frog and The One should see them before we leave.'

'I take it that you would be disappointed if you did not also go?' asked Katar.

'I can never visit Pelmore without going to the Hatcheries,' admitted Nadiah.

'If the truth be told, neither can I,' said Katar smiling. 'We have enough time before we meet Cassaria.'

They walked along several passageways and across small intersections until they finally turned a corner and came out onto a large square. In front of them was a pair of high wooden doors set into a stone archway. The dark, ebony-like wood was intricately carved with spiders of all shapes and sizes. In front of the doors stood half a dozen Pelmorian guards dressed in black robes set with a white spider insignia. Their faces were stern and serious.

Katar led the group forwards and as they approached, one of the guards spoke.

'We are honoured that Sand Master Katar visits us,

even in these troubled times.' He touched his forehead, bowed and stepped back as the other guards moved to either side. 'The doors are yours to open,' he announced.

Katar moved to the doors and pressed several of the individual carvings. Each one then silently moved across the face of the doors and found a new position in the pattern. He then turned and spoke to Frog and The One.

'Nadiah is well accustomed to the hatcheries, but as you have never been before I must instruct you on three things. Firstly, do not get separated from me. Secondly, make no quick movements or sudden noise and lastly, do not reach out and touch anything unless invited to do so. Is that clear?'

'Of course,' acknowledged The One.

Katar looked at Frog. 'Is that *clear*?' he emphasised.

'Perfectly,' confirmed Frog.

He turned back to the doors, a guard on either side pressed a small spider carving, and the great doors swung inwards.

Nadiah heard Frog and The One gasp out loud. Even she, after many visits, still found it hard to contain herself on entering the Hatcheries.

They were at the top of a flight of wide semi-circular steps, which allowed them to look out across the cavern and take in the view. Ahead of them and intertwined across the whole of the far wall hung an intricate pattern of silk spider's webs, which stretched up some 50 metres. The bluish light from the crystals shimmered and glistened along the strands of the web, each thread as thick as a man's arm. A dozen or so

Sandspiders were poised, motionless, as though defying gravity, across the astonishing feat of natural engineering. The enormity of it was truly breathtaking.

They made their way down the steps to the cave floor and Katar led them to the base of the structure where, in hollows of soft sand, individual grey-white objects about the size of large watermelons nestled.

'They're eggs!' exclaimed an excited Frog.

'I think the clue is the fact that we are in the *Hatcheries*,' said The One, not unkindly.

'But I thought that spiders built nests out of their silk and laid hundreds of eggs at a time,' said Frog.

'That may well be in your world,' said Nadiah. 'But, these are Sandspiders and as you know they can live for hundreds of years. Because of their longevity, they do not breed very often. In fact, a female Sandspider will lay just one egg every ten years.'

Frog looked up. 'I count about twelve Sandspiders, but there are only eight eggs. Are you waiting for the others to lay?'

'No,' replied Nadiah. 'They have already had their young if you look closely.' She pointed to one of the Sandspiders. 'You can just see the young one clinging on to its mother.'

They all took in the astounding sight until the Sandspider turned its position and the young spider was lost to them.

'Come,' said Katar. 'We have enough time to see the other spiderlings.'

They followed him to an antechamber where rows of small stables housed young Sandspiders. They were about half a metre in size and the fine hair on their bodies and legs was a golden brown. Several men and women, dressed in the now familiar robes, moved up and down, filling water bowls and food dishes. Some were cleaning out stalls.

A young woman sat brushing and grooming one of the spiderlings; its forelegs arched over her lap while the bulk of its body sat on the straw next to her. They watched, mesmerised, as the creature trembled with pleasure each time the brush passed across its back. It also made a soft, high-pitched purring noise that left no doubt about its delight.

'How old is it?' asked Frog.

'About eight months if I'm not mistaken,' answered Katar. 'They leave their mothers at six months and are introduced to a more solid diet.'

'Which is?' asked The One.

'Raw Saurs. They are, after all, carnivores,' said Katar.

'How long until they grow to full size?' enquired Frog.

'Ten years to maturity and during that time, at the training ground in Arachnae, they will choose and scent their rider and companion who will train them to hunt for themselves and to fight,' explained Katar. 'This is a very special relationship because a Sandspider usually outlives the rider who will eventually have to introduce and prepare a younger rider to take over. Some Sandspiders have as many as four dedicated riders during their lifetime.'

Nadiah nodded at them to look at Frog who was watching the young Sandspider intently. It may or may not have sensed his gaze but, at that moment, it shifted its position and turned to face him, the eight, liquid-black eyes focussing on him. It seemed that the Sandspider tilted its head with curiosity and then it moved forward slowly until it sat at his feet.

Katar put a finger to his lips and signalled for everyone to be quiet.

Frog knelt down and the Sandspider gently reached its two forelegs up and placed them on his chest; their faces were inches apart, the unblinking eyes of the Sandspider reflecting Frog's features. He rubbed the tops of its legs, letting the soft hairs run through his fingers and then he placed a hand just behind its head, caressing it as if he were stroking a cat behind its ears.

The purring went from a high pitch to a deep drone, reflecting the absolute bliss that the Sandspider was feeling. They were all lost in the moment when, suddenly, it stopped and the Sandspider quickly scuttled back to the lap of the young woman as if it has sensed some unseen threat.

Back in the large cavern, the giant Sandspiders tensed their many legs as a vibration rippled through the strands of their web.

'What's happening?' asked Frog, jumping to his feet.

'We must leave,' ordered Katar and turned quickly.

Nadiah and The One followed, but Frog paused for a moment and looked back at the young Sandspider. The girl now held a protective arm around it.

'Thank you,' he said.

He ran after the others and by the time he caught up with them, Katar was in conversation with one of the Pelmorian guards.

'There are tremors coming from the surface and upper levels,' said the guard. 'Whatever is causing them must be something very destructive for the effect to be felt at this depth.'

'When we leave, bring all of your men into the Hatcheries and seal the door behind you,' ordered Katar. 'I fear that Lord Maelstrom and his horde mean to bring the battle to us and are intent on destroying every part of Aridian.' He turned to the others. 'We must make haste to Cassaria. The time is quickly approaching when we will be needed.'

23

The Spear

Katar hurriedly took them back out to the plaza then down a short corridor until they came to a door, the image of a burning sun engraved at its centre.

'It's the sign of The Chosen!' exclaimed Frog. 'How did that get here?'

'Only the Guardian, Cassaria, can answer that for you,' replied Katar. 'I did not know of this place until she recently told me of its existence. All I am doing is following her instructions.'

He reached up, turned the image several times in different directions in much the same way, thought Frog, that you might undo a combination lock on a safe. There was a loud click and the sound of bolts withdrawing and then the door swung silently inwards. Katar beckoned them to step inside before following them and closing the door behind him. They were now in an oval room; at its centre were two semi-circular benches facing each other. A small crystal about the size of a fist was set into the centre of the floor, giving off an orange glow.

'Sit,' instructed Katar, taking his place on one of the benches.

Nadiah sat next to him while Frog and The One sat opposite, facing them.

'What now?' asked Frog.

'Now, I am to instruct you to push your sword into the crystal,' said Katar.

Frog drew his sword and they noticed that it gave off a soft golden glow of its own. He pushed the blade slowly into the crystal, which suddenly gave off a spectrum of orange and yellow lights. The ground beneath them gave a judder and the walls of the room fell away from around them to reveal a myriad of stars and a black velvet backdrop.

'What's happening?' shouted Nadiah.

'Hold on,' replied Frog. 'I think that we're going on a bit of a ride.'

The floor melted away in an instant, leaving the crystal floating in between them. They were then pushed upwards on a cushion of air and bright light; faster and faster they went until the stars around them dissolved into a blur.

'I can tell you from experience,' said Frog. 'Don't look down.'

'Whoa!' exclaimed The One as he tightly gripped the seat of the bench. 'There's nothing beneath us!'

'Yes, I know. I told you not to look down. Been there, done that.' Frog smiled as he looked across at Nadiah and Katar who were following his advice and keeping their heads turned firmly upwards.

Seconds passed by until the momentum gently slowed and darkness surrounded them. Then the stone floor, ceiling and the walls reconstructed themselves with a new doorway appearing.

'I guess that this is where we get off,' announced Frog, sheathing his sword.

'Not I,' said Katar remaining in his seat. 'I am to continue on to the surface and prepare my people. With good fortune we shall meet again soon.'

'Thank you for taking us to the Hatcheries,' said Frog. 'It's an experience that I will never forget.'

Katar nodded a thank you in return and they left him to continue his journey.

Nadiah led the rest of them to the door and tentatively pushed it open to reveal a simple, domed room. The stone floor was covered in runes and patterns. Cassaria stood next to a stone plinth on which sat the Hourglass and Rune Stone, surrounded by a glowing blue haze. Frog noticed that the sand in the Hourglass now filled two-thirds of the bottom chamber.

'Welcome,' said Cassaria. 'I understand that you have had some adventures since we were last together.'

'Nothing much really,' joked Frog. 'Just somebody trying to kill me again.'

'Trying to kill all of us,' added The One.

'Unfortunately, we will have to face worse,' said Cassaria. 'Events are moving faster than I could have foreseen. Belzeera and Lord Maelstrom have been using their foul Magic to create monstrous burrowing machines and are using them to try and penetrate the lower levels.'

'The cause of the tremors that we felt in Pelmore,' guessed Frog.

'I have used my Guardian's Magic to put a protective barrier around the lower levels of our communities, but it will not endure the attacks for very long. As we speak, Ameer moves the Aridian armies to the surface, to the Plain of Sighs for the defence of the Dimension. It is hoped that this will distract Lord Maelstrom and he will pull all of his resources together with the objective of defeating us first on the surface.'

'And what about us?' asked Nadiah. 'Is it now our time?'

'Indeed it is. Frog, you must stay close by my side. Our strength is with your sword, the Rune Stone and the Hourglass. I shall defend us all with whatever Magic that I can summon. Nadiah has the power of the Sisterhood to aid us.'

'And I have a bullwhip?' said The One with disappointment.

'You have something more than that, something much more powerful,' smiled Cassaria. 'The parchments on which the ancient Guardian symbols are written. Do you still have them?'

The One rummaged inside his robes and finally withdrew the rolled-up skins.

'I'm supposed to fight with these?' he asked, bemused.

'You have learnt the meaning of the symbols. You know their power. Study them well because when the time comes, your knowledge of them will be vital. You will also have need of this.'

She stretched her arms out over a particular circular rune on the floor and brought her gold bangles together. The centre of the rune began to ripple and liquidise. Slowly, a steel blue, metal tip began to rise up followed by a long wooden shaft until, finally, a spear hovered in the air in front of her.

'Take it,' she instructed The One.

He reached forward and grasped the spear as the floor returned to normal and Cassaria dropped her arms to release it into his grip.

'The Spear of Providence,' she said. 'A relic from the Guardians of old. It has their symbols on its shaft. You will need to interpret them for it to release its power and its purpose.'

The One studied the shaft of the spear and saw that there were four intricate markings etched into the wood. The sharp, flat iron spearhead also had the same four symbols engraved into the metal on either side.

He looked at the parchment and then to the spear.

'You want me to try and decipher it now?'

'As soon as you can, but whatever you do,' warned Cassaria, 'do not utter the words until the time is right.'

'How will I know when?'

'I will tell you. Now, we must complete the circle. Join hands with me around the Rune Stone.'

They formed a circle, holding hands.

'Breathe slowly,' she instructed. 'Close your eyes and empty your minds of all troubled thoughts.' The blue haze around the Rune Stone expanded outwards and around them all. 'I call upon the Magic of the Guardians and the power of the Rune Stone to protect us against the evils that we go to face. Bring us together and bind us in thought and deed and let it be seen that we have been embraced by its light.' Then she spoke in the ancient Magic tongue.

There was no bright, spectacular flash, but as the

213

blue haze receded back to the Rune Stone and they opened their eyes, the transformation in their attire was immediate for all to see.

Frog was clothed in robes of the deepest sea blue, while Nadiah's had turned to crimson. The One stood draped in colours of brown and green. Only Cassaria's robes remained an unchanged ice blue.

'Well, this is different,' said Frog inspecting himself. 'I would have preferred green.'

'These robes afford us some protection, but be aware; we are not immune to Lord Maelstrom's vile Magic,' said Cassaria. 'Now it is time for us to leave.'

She lifted the Rune Stone and the Hourglass from the plinth and led them all back through the door, to the now empty room where they sat down on the benches. This time she placed the Hourglass with the Rune Stone in its cradle onto the small crystal in the floor.

A blue haze filled the room and again the ground beneath them gave a shudder as the walls and the floor fell away around them. A warm breeze that rippled the material of their robes lifted them silently. There was no sense of speed, just the sensation of moving upwards.

It wasn't long before there was a slight jolt and the floor and walls reformed around them along with another doorway.

Cassaria picked up the Rune Stone and the Hourglass and led them out through the door, along a passage and to another door. As they followed her through it, they felt the temperature drop and saw that they were now in the small courtyard of a ruined and derelict building. Sand covered the floor and there were only two sections of crumbling wall left standing. It was night-time and the sky was full of stars. They moved out of the shadows and followed Cassaria, until they stood together, looking out. The panorama before them revealed itself under the light of the two, pale, featureless moons. They were now stood on a ridge of sand, some 20 metres high and overlooking a desert plain. The ridge arced away to their left for what seemed two or three miles. To their right at about a hundred metres from them was a break in the dune, a natural entrance on to the plain. Then the ridge resumed, curving back to run parallel with the other side. In the distance, a fortress stood dominating the far skyline, its twisted spires reaching into a black, swirling cloud that hovered menacingly. Spreading out from the fortress, they could see, even at this distance, large scattered fires burning, the flames licking at the sky and illuminating the incalculable army assembled there. Hoards of giant scorpions and indescribably twisted creatures with clawed and pincered weapons were gathered to the right and to the left. In the centre, legions of robed figures waited anxiously. Among them stood the great towering war machines.

'Dear Lord,' breathed The One.

'Those things in the wooden towers,' observed Frog. 'They look like giant corkscrews.'

'The tremors that we felt; that's what he's using,' said Nadiah. 'He is trying to burrow into the centre of Aridian itself, tunnelling down so that his army can invade our communities and cities.'

'Hopefully, we will have distracted him from that mission. The time draws near,' said Cassaria to Frog. 'He knows that we are here and he will come for you and the Rune Stone.'

24

Billy goes Bad

High on a balcony of the fortress, three figures stood looking out across the plain.

'They are here, my sister,' announced Lord Maelstrom. 'They think that they can defeat us with Guardian Magic. Well, we have a surprise for them don't we, my little friend?' He placed a hand on Billy's shoulder.

'Let me fly, brother,' said Belzeera eagerly. 'I can snatch the Stone and soak it in the boy's blood before they know what has happened. Let me be the one. Let me.'

'Patience! Speed is not of our concern. The weakness of the human heart will be their downfall. Now is the time for you to send out the diversion. Give orders to the Dreden that they are to send a small envoy across the plain. Tell them to deliver a message of choice – surrender or die!'

Belzeera stepped up onto the ledge and produced her wand. She flicked it in the air and floated out, her figure magically suspended high above the ground. With a nod of her head, she slowly spiralled down towards the waiting minions below.

Lord Maelstrom turned to Billy, whose face was white and ghostly, his dark eyes empty and soulless.

'You know what to do. It is your purpose. This is born of my Magic and when you strike, the power of your actions shall come to me,' he said as he concealed a small, black dagger in the folds of Billy's robes. Using the darkest of Magic, he touched Billy's head and the boy disintegrated into a small cloud of sand, which settled on Lord Maelstrom's open palm. Then, with glistening black lips, he blew it in the direction of Frog and the others, at the far end of the plain.

'Go, Earth Child. Bring me my prize. Bring me my destiny.'

He stretched his arms skyward and two bolts of lightning streaked down. His hands grasped the white-hot jagged plasma and he stood there laughing, his robes billowing around him. The air crackled with electricity and below, even the vile creatures of his making cowered and shivered with fear.

Frog, The One, Cassaria and Nadiah looked out at the lightning in the distance.

'Something dangerous and dark comes this way,' said Cassaria.

As she spoke, they could see a group of figures moving forwards on the plain. Jagged shards of blue electricity shot out over the Dreden, lighting up the creatures upon which they rode – giant, black scorpions.

'So it begins,' she added.

But, at that moment, Frog had something else troubling him. As much as he had tried to take his mind off it, he had been bursting to relieve himself for quite some time. He touched The One's arm.

'I've gotta go,' he said with a whisper. 'Be back in a minute.'

He hurried for the ruins and quickly found a place out of sight where, after struggling with his robes and with a sigh of relief, he managed eventually to empty his bladder. As he turned around, readjusting his clothes, a figure emerged from the shadows.

'Hiya Chris,' it whispered.

Apart from the colour of his robes, which were now black, the boy that stood in front of him was Frog's mirror image.

'Billy? Is it really you?' asked Frog.

'Of course it's me. Remember? I'm your best friend.'

His voice was flat, almost monotone and as he took a few steps forward, the moonlight glinted in his eyes and Frog saw the dark empty pupils.

'Billy, what's happened to you?'

'Help me, Chris. Help me,' he pleaded.

He reached out his hand and Frog moved towards him to take it. In the back of his mind, however, he wondered why Billy had called him Chris after everything he had been told. As Billy's hand clasped around his, a warning flashed through his mind, but it was too late. Billy's grip tightened and before Frog could counter-react, Billy had pulled him forward, sidestepped a leg behind him and pushed him back, all in one swift movement.

Frog lost his balance and fell backward to land heavily on the sand with Billy straddling his chest.

'What are you doing?' he asked with a gasp.

'My master's bidding,' rasped Billy as he brought out the dagger and pressed it to Frog's throat.

On the ridge, Cassaria turned to Nadiah and The One.

'Where's Frog?'

'He's had to go to the toilet. He's only over there behind a wall,' said The One.

'He was not to be separated, not to be alone,' she said, looking worriedly at the ruins. 'Go and get him, time is —' But before she could finish, they saw Frog step out, Billy behind him, one hand pressing the knife at Frog's throat, the other holding him in an arm lock.

Nadiah brought her arms forwards, hands glowing blue.

'No!' said Cassaria. 'Don't move. Let him tell us what he wants.'

'Don't hurt him,' pleaded Frog. 'Something's taken him over, but he's still my best friend. He's still Billy.'

The One stood captivated by Billy's transformation. 'It's like looking at twins.'

Billy's face showed no emotion as he and Frog shuffled forwards to within a couple of metres of Cassaria.

'So much for my Taekwondo training,' said Frog. 'Tricked by one of the easiest moves in the book. I can't believe that I was so stupid.'

'Shut up!' shouted Billy.

Cassaria took a step forward and Billy increased the pressure on Frog's arm.

'I don't think that he wants you to do that,' grimaced Frog.

'What do you want?' she asked.

'The Stone. Give me the Stone,' Billy demanded his voice now deep and guttural.

'Of course,' she said. 'Here, take it.'

She held the Hourglass out with the Rune Stone set into its top.

'No! You can't,' shouted The One. 'He'll kill him.'

'Take it,' encouraged Cassaria, holding it out closer to him.

Billy released the grip on Frog's arm and stretched his hand forwards whilst keeping the knife close to Frog's throat with his other hand. The Rune Stone was only a fingertip away from his grasp. Then, several things happened in quick succession; Frog took the opportunity to grab Billy's knife hand, bringing it up above his head, whilst sidestepping and twisting Billy's arm behind his back. His grip on the dagger loosened and it fell to the floor.

Billy screamed with rage. A deep demonic groan, rising into a thunderous roar, escaped from his wide-open mouth.

'Noooooooooooooooooooooooooooooooooooooo!'

Nadiah let loose a shock wave from one of her hands, which hit Billy squarely in the chest. The force knocked him backwards into Frog so that they both fell to the floor. As Billy scrabbled to free himself, Cassaria moved forward. She thrust the Hourglass at Billy so that the Rune Stone was pressing against his chest. His body went rigid as blue light enveloped it.

'Leave this boy, vile monster,' she shouted. 'You want to feel the power of the Rune Stone? Then you shall feel it through him.'

Frog rolled away to one side and The One helped him up and pulled him to safety.

'Don't kill him. Don't kill him,' pleaded Frog desperately.

Billy's mouth opened and a green mist poured out. It formed the shape of a face in the air above them, the features becoming quickly recognisable as Lord Maelstrom.

'I shall have his blood!' the spectre boomed, then the image distorted and the green vapour streaked out and across the plain towards the dark tower.

Cassaria knelt beside Billy's prostrate body and Frog pulled himself from The One's arms and threw himself down next to them.

'You've killed him,' he sobbed, taking hold of Billy's cold and lifeless hand.

'I have saved his soul, but you must save his life,' said Cassaria. She took a small flask from her robe and, gently opening Billy's mouth, poured in an amber liquid. The transformation was almost immediate. Frog's features faded and melted away to reveal Billy's true appearance and identity. Colour returned to his face and hands, but he remained in a lifeless coma.

'You must take him home,' said Cassaria. 'Not until he is back in your Dimension can you restore his mind.'

'Why can't I do it here?' asked Frog.

'He cannot take the memories of what he has been subjected to here back into your Dimension. They would drive him insane in an instant. You must take him back to the point of his entry into the Slipstream, to the place that you left. Then and only then can you save him.'

'And how do I do that?'

'Through the power of The Chosen. Use it on Billy as you used it on me. Let the light deliver him from evil.'

222

She stood up and held out the Hourglass. 'Draw your sword and hold his hand.'

Frog did as he was told.

'You must be swift. When you have administered the healing to Billy, you must leave him. He will awaken when you have gone and remember nothing.'

'But what about his clothes?' asked The One.

'Trust me,' said Cassaria. 'All will be as it should be. Now, place your sword onto the Rune Stone.'

Frog hesitated. 'How do I get back?'

'The same way that you came here – free sand. Be quick as time will continue to move faster here.'

Frog rested the flat of the sword's blade onto the Rune Stone. He looked at The One and Nadiah.

'See you soon,' he said and the blue light ran down the length of the sword and into his arm, engulfing both him and Billy until, with bright flash, they were gone.

The whirling space and shooting lights of the Slipstream carried them along and spun them into its dark cloak. When Frog opened his eyes, he was back behind the shed in the murky shadows of his own garden. As he sat up, he looked at Billy who lay quietly beside him.

'Sorry mate. Sorry that I got you into such a mess and sorry that you won't be able to remember how brave and loyal you were. At least I know how much of a true and courageous friend you are.'

He leant over and gently touched Billy's forehead. The familiar glow of Castellion's Chosen reached out from Frog's forehead and into Billy's brow until, after a while, it faded away and Frog could see that Billy was breathing gently and rhythmically. He took comfort to see the peaceful expression on Billy's face, which was almost a smile. He then patted Billy's arm and stood up.

'I'll see you again my friend. I'm going to fix that evil creep for good. I'll teach him to mess around and hurt my best mate.' He checked his watch – 17.48. He then turned to the sand that he had spilled onto the ground earlier and plunged his sword into it. The Slipstream opened up and swallowed him, drawing him in until the moment that its darkness clouded his senses.

25

The Battle for Aridian

When Frog awoke, he opened his eyes to find Nadiah kneeling beside him.

'Welcome back. Are you all right? Is Billy all right?'

'I'm okay thanks, but I'm not sure about Billy,' he replied getting to his feet. 'Where's The One and Cassaria?'

'Over on the ridge. They asked me to wait here for your return.'

'How long have I been gone?'

'Long enough. Come and see.'

He got up, brushed the sand from his robes and followed her. He ducked his head in surprise, as there was a sudden flash of lightning and two silhouettes were lit up in front of him. The sky trembled with thunder and as he reached the ridge, he stood shocked at the view laid out on the plain below.

'Nice to have you back. How's Billy?' asked The One.

'Breathing and looking a lot better when I left him. Where did this lot come from?'

About a mile from them was an army of human and inhuman shapes, covering the plain right back as far as the fortress.

'There must be thousands of them,' said Frog.

'And many more yet to be seen,' said Cassaria.

'How did they manage to cover the ground so quickly,' he asked.

'Many hours have passed while you travelled the Slipstream,' she replied.

Frog looked at his watch. 17.48.

'Three minutes; that's all it was. Three minutes. It's like having an out of control time machine,' he said, exasperated.

'Focus on the now,' she instructed. 'Take your positions at arm's length to each other. Frog to my left. The One to my right and Nadiah next to Frog.'

'We're not taking this lot on alone, are we?' asked The One.

Cassaria did not answer, but placed the Hourglass on the sand at her feet. She brought her wrists together and the bangles glowed white-hot until a beam, like a searchlight, shot up from them into the sky.

As they looked out, figures began to rise up along the sand dunes on either side of the plain. The great Sandspiders of Aridian and their riders filled each horizon, their metal harnesses glinting in the moonlight. The riders sat high on the spider's backs. Each one held a small crossbow in their hands at the ready and Frog could make out racks of long spears and arrows fixed to the harnesses.

Close to their left, they could see Ameer, his white robe rippling in a sudden breeze. Opposite him on the other ridge was the dark figure of Katar sitting astride a two-tone, black and white Sandspider. Amongst this welcome army were hundreds of white pennants and flags, each one emblazoned with the black spider insignia of Aridian.

Frog caught a movement from the corner of his eye and looked towards the gap in the dunes to their right. Rows and rows of orange-robed figures began to emerge and move forward, spreading out across the desert floor.

'The Sisterhood,' acknowledged Nadiah. 'I should be with them,' she added wistfully.

They watched as the Sisterhood filled the plain in front of them until nearly two thousand orange figures stood, facing the direction of Lord Maelstrom's army.

'Some of them look so young,' said The One.

'Do not let their youth deceive you,' said Cassaria. 'They have courage beyond their years.'

The light from Cassaria's bangles turned yellow, a roar went up from the lines of Sandspiders and they started their descent, down the steep dunes and into conflict.

Jagged shards of lightning traced across the sky, turning everything monochrome with its strobe effect and momentarily blinding anyone who looked at it. Groups of Dreden broke away from the main army and rushed to meet the oncoming Sandspiders, while the legions of ugly, twisted creatures pushed forwards to attack the Sisterhood. The clamour and confusion of battle ensued as the Dreden and the Sandspiders clashed.

The sudden speed at which Lord Maelstrom's vile creations advanced on the Sisterhood was unexpected, propelling them forward onto a collision course.

'What are they?' asked Frog.

'More likely, what *were* they?' corrected Nadiah. 'There is some resemblance amongst them of desert animals and insects, but goodness knows what awful things have been done to transform them into these abominable beings.'

Cassaria's bangles now sent out a deep orange light and with the change in colour, the Sisterhood formed two ranks, the first about 2 metres in front of the other, their arms outstretched and their fists glowing blue-white.

Closer and closer the swarm came and not one of the Sisterhood flinched until, with only a few metres remaining, the first line opened their palms and the shock waves rippled out. The result was devastating. The creatures exploded and disintegrated into dust, row upon row of them nine or ten deep. The next line of Sisterhood stepped forwards and repeated the exercise to the same effect and so they advanced, cutting into the mass, turning the enemy into fine particles, which dropped to the ground to be trampled underfoot and mixed into the sand.

On the sand dunes either side, the Sandspiders were advancing steadily down, their riders firing their crossbows with deadly accuracy. Dreden fell dead before they could reach the Sandspider's legs with their swords and spears.

Cassaria lowered her arms and the bangles returned to normal, but lightning continued to streak out from the tower to illuminate the whole plain.

'We seem to be defeating them on all sides of our attack,' said The One.

'Look.' said Nadiah. 'The Sisterhood are forcing the creatures back into the paths of the Sandspiders.'

The creatures were now in a confused panic, turning on each other in an effort to run from the power of the Sisterhood. Behind them, Dreden were caught in the chaotic retreat and found themselves being attacked by the dreadful creations. Very soon, the Sandspiders were upon them all, the riders now using the long-handled spears to keep at bay and dispatch their enemies, the Sandspiders using their forelegs to pick up any adversary that got within reach, piercing them with sharp fangs before throwing the bodies back into the fighting, scrabbling mass.

'This is too easy,' said Cassaria. 'Something's wr –' But before she could finish, a deafening roll of thunder, which shook the ground, drowned out her voice and great holes appeared along the surrounding dunes. Many of the Sandspiders disappeared into the deep fissures, their legs scrabbling for purchase as the quicksand dragged them down with their riders. The fast-running sand spread out claiming many more victims before finally closing in on top of them and sealing their fate in suffocating tombs. Large gaps in the ranks of Aridian's army now made them vulnerable to counterattack.

The Sisterhood had pushed their way into the centre of the battle and were fighting in all directions. Many casualties were indeed amongst the younger, less-experienced students, who had depleted their power and had lost the energy to recharge and defend themselves.

Elsewhere, Ameer found himself surrounded.

Blackened creatures clawed and bit into his Sandspider's legs and it hissed with pain and rage. One large, long-legged half-insect, half-lizard leapt onto the Sandspider's back. Its mantis-like mandibles snapped open and lunged forward, narrowly missing Ameer's neck. With a spear in each hand, he focussed on fighting off two ugly lizards, intent on tearing at his Sandspider's eyes and was unaware of the dreadful thing behind him as it drew its head back for a second strike. It had moved closer and this time was certain of success. Once again, the jaws opened ready to sever Ameer's head from his body but, instead, an arrow flew into its neck. Green blood splashed out and the creature crumpled sideways. Ameer looked to see it fall into the scrabbling figures below. A second arrow also found its mark and one of the lizards fell lifeless at the spider's feet. Ameer turned to see where it had come from and saw a smiling Katar, loading up another arrow.

Ameer touched his forehead in thanks and turned back to look around him. It seemed to him that the Sandspiders and the Sisterhood were holding their ground against their adversaries, but not without many casualties. He wondered how much longer they could stave off the onslaught when the deep boom of war-drums echoed out.

From the base of the towers, they came. The giant, black, glistening scorpions swarmed out and around the sides of the plain. Their intention was clear: to encircle the battle and trap the Aridian army who would then have no means of escape and nowhere to turn. The snapping, riderless creatures quickly completed their task. They froze, their tails arced and their hooked stings dripping green poison as they waited for a command.

'They'll cut our people to ribbons,' said Nadiah.

'Have faith,' replied Cassaria. Again, she brought the bangles together and an emerald green beam reached upwards.

This time, a blue glow began to radiate along the high ridges of the dunes. To their left, a lone figure appeared riding a Sandspider. He was dressed in the white robes of Aridian. One hand gripped a tall standard bearing the flag of Aridian; a sudden breeze unfurled the image for all to see. In his other hand, he held a long bladed scimitar, which he raised above his head. Slowly, white turbaned heads began to appear, rising up, their numbers spilling out over the sand and passing all expectations.

Baron and his followers spread out, their ranks joined by many more Sandspiders. Glowing rock crystals hung like medallions from their harnesses.

Frog saw Baron stand on his spider's saddle. He brought his curved sword forward; the blade glinted from the moonlight and a roar went up. The Sand-spiders moved slowly down the dunes, crisscrossing each other's paths as they released long strands of spider silk, which created a meshed web behind them. Then scores of the Dreden allies rushed forwards with long bows. They produced arrows with thin threads of silk already attached, which they tied to the web, then they finally set their arrows into position and stood, ready to fire.

The scorpions sensed a threat and turned to face the

oncoming Sandspiders, but they were too late. The arrows were released, lifting the web over the heads of the Sandspiders to drop onto the giant, black, venomous scorpions. The sticky substance of the fresh web stuck to the bodies and as they snapped and twisted to escape, they became more entangled with each move. Then Baron's Dreden army were upon them. The Sandspiders reared up, pushing with their forelegs to lift the scorpions and expose the soft, vulnerable underbellies, which they immediately attacked with spears, swords and arrows.

One of the creatures managed to cut through enough of the web to free itself and Katar, who was nearby, turned his Sandspider and joined the efforts to stop the beast. He leapt down and sliced into one of the skeletal legs and then another. A pincer arm swung down, snapping at the air in search of Katar, who sidestepped and brought the great blade of his scimitar swinging around in an arc to sever the claw from its owner. The creature emitted an ear-splitting scream as it lost its balance and toppled sideways giving Baron's men the chance to drive their spears home and put an end to it.

Even as it died, it carried out one last wicked deed. The tail flipped forwards and the poisonous sting struck Katar in his back. His death was mercifully instantaneous, but went unnoticed in the clamour of battle.

Lord Maelstrom's army was in disarray. With the arrival of Baron's reinforcements, there had been a new vigour in the Aridian army as they sensed that victory was within their reach. But the battle was far from over.

Another sudden roll of thunder shook the skies, followed by a further streak of lightning, and on a blade of electric current, Belzeera rode out, her arms outstretched, her long black clothes shimmering with static. She swooped above the throng, flicking her wand down and releasing blue thunderbolts of raw energy into the Sisterhood. Several of them directed their power at the witch, but she seemed protected against the force as if surrounded by a hidden shield.

Nadiah turned away, tears in her eyes. 'Do something,' she pleaded to Cassaria. 'She will destroy them all.'

'The witch's greed for power will be her downfall,' said Cassaria. 'Keep the spear close to your side and be ready to throw straight and true,' she instructed The One.

'Touch your brow, young Frog. Let the light of The Chosen flow forth.'

Without question, he did as he was told and the shining sun of The Chosen appeared on his forehead. The golden rays stretched out, changing the colour of the very air around them. As the illumination spread towards her, Belzeera looked up and an expression of greed filled her face. She turned away from her evil business and sped towards the little group.

'Join hands with me now,' commanded Cassaria as Belzeera came to a halt a few metres above them, floating on her electric blue platform.

She pointed her black, twisted wand at Frog.

'Pick up the Hourglass and step forwards,' she ordered.

He felt Cassaria's hand tighten around his and he stood his ground.

'You dare defy me?' spat the witch with rage.

'We all defy you,' replied Cassaria. 'Fire, water, air and earth.' As she spoke each word, the colours of their robes radiated intensely: Nadiah – red; Frog – deep blue; Cassaria – ice blue; The One – green and brown.

The lightning shard supporting Belzeera blackened and cracked. Her brow furrowed and doubt crossed her face.

'Now,' said Cassaria in almost a whisper, but The One heard her clearly.

He moved his hand away from his side and revealed the spear. The symbols on the shaft and blade shone white-hot.

Fear crossed Belzeera's face, an emotion that she had never felt before as The One threw the spear. Belzeera pointed her wand, but it was immediately torn from her grasp. It flew towards the hourglass, passing the spear on its way. Thunder boomed overhead and as it echoed along the plain, the spear reached the witch and stopped, poised, just centimetres from her breast.

She looked down at the pointed blade, its symbols glowing molten. A trembling smile crossed her lips and she exhaled a nervous laugh.

'Ha! The old Magic fails you.'

The One's voice spoke clear and strong.

'Fallah. Rania. Hevas. Erith.'

The spear pierced her robe; the blade disappeared into her body followed by the long shaft. However, it did not exit through her. It was absorbed into her.

Her image stretched and warped. She thrashed and clawed at the air around her and a network of fine, dark cracks spread out across the skin of her face. Her eyes bulged as she felt the final fear and recognition that her end was upon her. Her mouth opened into a silent scream before she imploded into nothingness.

Her wand hovered above the Rune Stone, still set into the top of the Hourglass and Cassaria reached forward with one hand and pushed it downwards. As it touched the Rune Stone, it fragmented into thousands of pieces, which changed from black, to blue and the slivers melted into the Rune Stone itself.

At that moment, a thunderous roar shook the ground with the force of an earthquake, knocking them off their feet. In the distance, blood-red flames shot out of the fortress and a firestorm of lightning erupted in the sky. Black and crimson clouds formed overhead, blotting out the stars and twin moons. The pure light that came from Frog's brow reached out and pushed back the darkness. They all watched as the fortress shook and its pinnacles and balconies crumbled, falling into a mushroom-shaped cloud of dust. Then, from the billowing debris, the deafening voice of Lord Maelstrom boomed.

'By killing my sister you have doomed this Dimension. I shall destroy you all. There will be no mercy. Empty desolation is all that shall remain of this wretched world. Behold, I am come and all shall suffer my wrath.'

The figure, which emerged from the dust cloud, was a monstrous demon, over 10 metres in height. There was no doubt that it was Lord Maelstrom, but his whole being was on fire, even his ragged trailing robes. Flames danced across the material, rippled over his skin; his face burned and moved like the surface of the sun.

He stepped forwards, crushing his own wicked creations beneath his feet. Molten fire dripped from his fingers and fell around him, burning like brimstone, incinerating anything that came into contact.

Every living thing on that plain – men, women, Sandspiders, even the things of his own and Belzeera's making – turned and ran, scattering out in all directions with one purpose – survival.

26

Blood on the Stone

Frog opened his mind, to let the evil of Lord Maelstrom enter, forcing back the dreadful, despicable and vile thoughts and images that tried to push through and corrupt him.

'You want me? Come and get me,' he shouted mentally.

In the distance, Lord Maelstrom's head snapped up. 'Let us finish this now,' he bellowed back.

He strode across the plain, his sheer size helping him to cover the ground in a matter of moments. He stretched out a fiery arm and pointed towards the little group on the dune.

'This will be the greatest pleasure of all. Prepare to die, Guardian. You will not live to see me turn these meddling fools into empty, soulless servants.'

Cassaria picked up the Hourglass. The last few grains of sand were falling into the bottom.

'You forgot your greatest enemy,' she said.

She turned the Hourglass on its side and time instantly stood still around them. All movement ceased and the battlefield was frozen. Even the demonic Lord Maelstrom remained immobile.

The Rune Stone suddenly released itself and dropped from the cradle. With a reflex action, The One reached out and caught it before it dropped to the ground.

Even when everything was over, he could not explain what prompted him to do what he did next.

He took out the parchments and wrapped them around the Rune Stone then he threw the package with all his might at the towering Lord Maelstrom, shouting out the words again.

'Fallah. Rania. Hevas. Erith.'

It flew forwards through the air, struck the evil sorcerer on the chest, and then attached itself to him. The glow of the Rune Stone shone through the parchment and spread out across his body, turning crimson red to bright blue. As they watched, the figure of Lord Maelstrom began to shrink, slowly at first and then the momentum accelerated until he returned to his normal size.

The Hourglass twisted in Cassaria's hands. It turned upright, the sand now in the top chamber. Grains started to drop through the narrow gap and time started again. Black and crimson clouds continued to billow out and fill the sky. Lord Maelstrom reached to his chest and took hold of the Rune Stone, still wrapped in the ancient parchment. Now, there was no glow, no radiance. He extended his other hand and a black wand appeared in it.

'Did you think that you could stop me? Your end has finally come, Guardian.'

He flicked the wand at her, but nothing happened. He tried again to no effect then looked at the wand with a puzzled expression.

'Your powers are gone,' said Cassaria. 'You are mortal.'

Rage filled his face. He shook the Rune Stone in anger, raising it in the air and meaning to dash it on the ground when, suddenly, he stared at the parchment.

'There is blood,' he smiled. He tore the material open. 'There is blood on the Stone!'

The One looked at his hand; a smear of blood trailed across his palm. Protruding from his skin, he saw a small wooden splinter, which had broken off from the spear's shaft as he had thrown it at Belzeera.

'The blood of the father is enough!' screeched Lord Maelstrom in crazed triumph.

He brought his wand hand up to his mouth and bit into his own flesh, tearing open the skin and letting his blood drip onto the stone and mix with The One's.

'This will be enough, Guardian. The parchment; it is organic. This will take me to the Third Dimension. I will find a way to rise up again.' He looked menacingly at Frog. 'I will find your world, boy, and I will bring the endless night and deliver eternal torment. I will take the souls of your father and mother as trophies and you shall be my slave for all eternity.'

'Stop him,' shouted Frog.

'Nothing can stop him,' said Cassaria. 'He has the Rune Stone in his power. We must let him go.'

As they watched, the Rune Stone regained its radiance, which then spread into Lord Maelstrom. The air in front of him rippled and a tear appeared, a rip in the very fabric of time and space. Through this, a glimpse of darkness and scattered stars was seen

239

before he was drawn in and the entrance to the Slipstream sealed behind him.

'Use your Magic,' pleaded Frog. 'Let's follow him and end it once and for all.'

Cassaria turned to Frog. 'There are older, more ancient forces at work here that arranged his escape. We have done as much as we can in this Dimension. Whatever destiny has designed for you, it will be revealed in some other place, in some other time. You are not meant to follow. Not yet.'

'Look,' shouted Nadiah and she pointed at the yellow-tinted skyline. 'Sunrise will soon be upon us.'

Down on the plain, with Lord Maelstrom gone, the Aridian army regrouped and confronted what was left of his followers. The mutated creatures fought with renewed frenzy, but they were no match for Ameer's men and the Sandspiders. Some of the Dreden continued to fight while many of them surrendered to Baron's supporters, laying down their weapons and kneeling in submission.

The scene was now illuminated by a new dawn, which shone out in rays from under the great black clouds that covered the expanse of the plain. The clouds thundered yet again and blue-white electricity rippled through the dark undulating mass.

'What now?' asked Nadiah. 'Have we not seen enough horrors?'

'It is the aftermath of Lord Maelstrom's sorcery,' replied Cassaria. 'But perhaps some good can come of its presence. Who has a water bottle?'

The One produced a small leather canteen. Cassaria stretched out her arms and brought the bangles together.

'Pour the water over them, quickly,' she instructed. The One pulled out the stopper and did as he was told. As the liquid flowed over them, the bangles turned blue and a thin shaft of light shot out into the threatening storm above them. The clouds began to boil and churn, spreading out in all directions until the sky was overcast for as far as the eye could see. The two suns broke over the horizon, their light and heat flooding out and into the new dark canopy. Then it happened. One small drop of water landed on Frog's upturned face. He wiped it away with his fingers before several others landed around them, large, fat droplets making dark splash marks in the sand.

Out on the plain in the now strange light, the fighting had stopped; all faces looked skyward as the heavens opened.

'Rain!' shouted Nadiah, holding her arms out, her clothes soaking up the downpour.

Frog watched her face light up with a smile, with sheer happiness.

'Will this last?' asked The One.

Cassaria looked out onto the Plain of Sighs.

'For once his sorcery has been used for the good,' she said. 'From Lord Maelstrom's dark creation comes a change to Aridian. It will return life to the surface. It will give its people choice. Sadly, it has been bought at such a cost.' The rain drenched her face, concealing the tears that fell from her eyes.

It rained non-stop for ten days. The heat of the twin suns and the mix of black and white Magic had created a new, stronger atmosphere for Aridian and a healthy weather system developed. Lakes started to form and in the rocky outcrops, plant life appeared, rising out of the once-parched land.

Over the coming days and weeks, old wounds were healed, comrades and kinsmen were mourned, meetings were held and councils formed until finally, early one warm evening, there was another great gathering on the Plain of Sighs. This time its nature was peaceful.

They assembled in circles, thousands of them, amidst the white, cottony clouds decorating a powder blue sky. The heat from the suns was a bearable temperature as their light now shone through a protective haze.

Dreden stood side by side with Aridian and Sisterhood. The colours of their robes were orange, blue, brown, white and black. Each one now bore the Sandspider insignia. At the centre of the inner circle was the Hourglass on a stone plinth. Gathered around it were Cassaria, Frog, The One, Nadiah, Ameer and Baron. Frog was dressed once again in his green medieval clothes.

Cassaria's voice rang out clear for all to hear.

'A new chapter begins for Aridian. We have defended and reclaimed our Dimension and repelled the evil that threatened us. Our history shall be our future as once again we are a united people. Let us now remember our fallen.'

Every single figure knelt on one knee, bowed their heads and remained hushed for a minute before Cassaria broke the silence.

'To continue the unity and hope that binds us, Prince Ameer and Baron will lead you on your journey to fully reclaim Aridian's surface and Nadiah of the Sisterhood will take the fallen Katar's place as Sand Master of the Sandspiders. I will continue to act as guide, counsel and Guardian. The Hourglass will remain here and shall be housed in a structure of peace and remembrance. Whosoever has the duty to turn it in a thousand years will know the sacrifices that gave us our freedom.'

As the suns touched the horizon and the gathering disbanded, Ameer and Baron gave their heartfelt thanks to Frog and The One.

'We shall never forget the bond between our worlds,' said Ameer to Frog. 'You answered the call in our hour of need and I am joyful that we were able to reunite you with your father. We are indebted to you both.'

Baron took Frog's hand.

'I am saddened for your friend, that he will not have the memories of his courage or have anyone speak to him of his bravery and loyalty. I can only tell you that when I have a son he shall be given the name of Billy.'

Frog smiled. 'He'd like that, I'm sure.'

Ameer and Baron touched their foreheads and chests in salute before turning and making their way to their waiting Sandspiders.

Nadiah turned to Frog and he could see that she was holding back tears.

'To some, we are children. However, many, many adults have not endured what we have had to face and are never likely too. I am old enough to understand what I feel in my heart and I am saddened to be losing you. Remember, we are only a Slipstream apart.' She reached inside the folds of her orange and black robes.

'This is from Arac-Khan.' She took his arm and clipped a black bracelet, fashioned in the shape of a Sandspider, around his wrist. 'It will give you a kinship with spiders everywhere.' She took Frog's hands in hers. 'This is from me,' she said and leaned forwards to kiss him tenderly on each cheek. She then threw her arms around him and hugged him tightly. He hugged her back, enjoying their embrace.

After a few moments, she pulled herself away and Frog could see the tracks of two tears running down her cheeks.

'Goodbye,' she whispered.

Frog stood there, his heart in his mouth, as she walked away towards a waiting Sandspider. She climbed up into the seat and rode off without looking back.

He felt a hand rest gently on his shoulder.

'Time to go home.' It was his father's voice.

'Take out your sword, young Frog,' said Cassaria. 'Place it on the Hourglass to open the Slipstream.'

'I still think that we should go after Lord Maelstrom,' he said.

'When you are needed, you will be called,' said Cassaria. 'As your father said, it is time to go home. Once again, the Guardians are in debt to you. You have become everything that has been expected of the legend that is Frog, but you have another life, for now. Go and enjoy the reunion of your family.'

The One smiled at Cassaria then clasped his hand around Frog's as the sword touched the Hourglass. The Slipstream opened up and pulled them in.

27

Home

Chris opened his eyes. He was on his back, staring up into to a starry night sky. He eased himself slowly up, taking in his surroundings; he was back home in the garden. The pile of sand lay next to him. He looked at his watch – 17.48.

His father was nowhere to be seen.

'Dad?' he called. 'Dad?'

There was no answer.

Now what? he thought.

Resisting the urge to panic, he hurried to the shed and stepped inside, closing the door behind him as he switched on the dim light. He opened the dresser drawer and hid the garments and items from his travels. When he tried to remove the spider bracelet, however, he was astounded to find that it had melted into his skin and become a black tattoo.

'Oh. Great,' he said as he ran his fingers across the pattern, 'I hope that this is like my finger and can't be seen by anyone else.'

He quickly changed into his normal clothes and then hurried around the corner of the house to the kitchen door. As he pushed it open, he could hear his mother's tears. She sat crying at the table, her face in her hands.

'Mum. What's wrong?' He ran to her and put his arms around her.

She lifted her head, smiling through her tears. 'It's your dad. They've found him. He's coming home, Chris. He's coming home.'

His mother went on to tell him that she had just received a telephone call from the British Embassy in Morocco. His father had been found wandering around on a desert road near the city of El Ayun. He was safe and well but, as a precaution, he was being checked over by doctors at the local hospital. As soon as they had more news, they would ring her.

Chris could not contain his excitement. The boy in him had returned.

'Let's go to the airport now,' he shouted. 'Let's get a plane out and bring him home.'

'It doesn't work like that,' said his mum. 'We have to be patient. Let's wait for the phone call.' She got up and wiped her face with a tissue. 'I need a strong cup of tea,' she said and filled the kettle.

Chris wanted to tell her everything, but he knew deep down inside that he couldn't. It would do no good and just complicate things. He just needed to focus on his father's return.

Will he remember what happened on Aridian? he wondered. *How will he react when he sees me?* Then, he thought of Billy. How could he have forgotten about Billy?

'Just going upstairs a minute,' he announced.

When he got to his bedroom, he closed the door. With trembling hands, he picked up his mobile phone, brought up Billy's name on the screen and hit the call button. All he got was a message saying that the connection was unobtainable. He pressed the cancel button and keyed in Billy's home number.

After three rings, Billy's mum answered.

'Hello, Mrs Smart,' said Chris with a slightly nervous voice. 'Is Billy there?'

'Hi Chris. I think that he's up in his room,' she replied. 'I'll just get him.'

Chris heard her call for Billy, followed by muffled voices and after a few moments, she returned.

'He's tucked himself up in bed, Chris. He doesn't feel very well. It sounds like he's coming down with something. It's probably just a cold. I'll get him to ring you tomorrow if he's better.'

'Thanks, Mrs Smart.' Chris switched off his phone. He would just have to wait to talk to Billy, but at least he knew that his best friend was alive.

Later that evening, his mum received another call. This time it was from his dad. Chris stood beside her as she cried and told her husband how much she loved him and how she missed him. After a while, she passed the phone to Chris.

'Hi Dad. How are you?'

'Fine. Fine apart from a nice scar on my head.'

'Can you remember anything?'

'Not much apart from falling into a hole, lots of dust and then standing on a road looking at some lights in the distance. Apparently, I've been gone for quite a while. They seem to think that some tribe of nomads have been looking after me because when I was found, I was dressed in Bedouin clothes.'

'And that's it?'

'Yes. Why do you ask?'

Chris held his breath.

'Chris? What's wrong?'

'Nothing. Nothing. When are you coming home?'

'They're putting me on a flight home tomorrow. I should be back by late evening your time.'

'I love you, Dad.'

'I love you too, son. Look, I'm sorry that I don't have much time so we'll speak tomorrow. Can you put your mum back on?'

'Sure.'

He passed the phone back to his mother and got himself a coke from the fridge. His head was spinning. How could his dad forget Aridian and was Billy really going to be all right?

After a restless night, Chris woke up late, but before he even had his breakfast or brushed his teeth, he phoned Billy's home again.

After half a dozen rings, the phone was answered.

'Hello?' said a hoarse voice.

'Billy?' said Chris.

'Hi Chris. How you doing?' Billy croaked.

'Never mind me. How are you?'

'I'm okay. I've just got a really sore throat.'

'Is that all?' said Chris.

'Why, were you expecting more?'

'No. No. I'm just glad that you're okay. I expected to see you yesterday, that's all.'

'Well, here's a weird thing,' said Billy. 'All I remember is getting ready to come around then, all of a sudden, I was lying in bed with a thumping headache.

Mum gave me some medicine and I went out like a light. I had some really crazy dreams though. Giant spiders and things. Ugh!'

'As long as you're okay.'

'Yeah. But I reckon that I can get a week off school with this,' he said laughing hoarsely. 'Anyhow, I hear they found your dad. That's gotta be brilliant.'

'How do you know that?' asked Chris.

'It's all over the news. I saw it on the telly about half an hour ago.'

'Gotta go, Billy. Speak to you later,' Chris apologised.

He rushed downstairs and passed the news to his mother before turning on the television. Sure enough, there were regular reports about his father's miraculous return and they spent the rest of the day flashing through the news channels watching in fascination as the story attracted comments and speculation.

By the time Chris's father reached home, every national newspaper was after his story and an interview. In fact, when he reached the front door, he had to fight his way past the photographers to get in, politely asking them to respect his own and his family's privacy. Among a flurry of camera flashes, his wife opened the door and let him in, quickly shutting it safely behind her.

The three of them stood there in the hall, hugging each other for a long time. Eventually they released their embrace, but chose to sit at the foot of the stairs in conversation. Chris's mum tenderly inspected the scar on her husband's head and examined his sun-tanned and careworn face, her tears and kisses a testament of her deep love for him. Chris held his father's hand, not wanting to let go. They stayed like this for a long time, a silence and warmth of emotion shielding them from any other thoughts, bringing them together again as a family.

Later, after his dad had showered and was sitting on the bed in his bathrobe, towelling his thick dark hair, Chris came in and sat next to him. He brought him up to date with his progress at school and told him how he had gained another two belts at Taekwondo.

'You know how very proud I am of you,' said his dad as he playfully threw the damp towel at him. As he did so, however, the top of his bathrobe opened to reveal a pendant hanging around his neck.

Chris stared open-mouthed as he took in the detail of a small, black spider suspended on a silver chain.

'Where … Where did you get that?'

'This?' he asked holding it between his fingers. 'That's a whole different story,' he said with a wink and left the room.

Epilogue

The Third Dimension ...

A steamy rainforest; the air reverberates with a wild chorus of nature echoing down from the tropical canopy and up from the lush damp undergrowth. Trees and plants glisten, dew-dropped and moist with the humid environment. Shafts of light streak through tall, long-limbed trees to reflect from broad leaves and invade patches of shaded groves.

Rising up in the distance is the snow-capped peak of a dormant volcano. There is the laughter of children, playing somewhere in the vegetation. This is a strange paradise where bright colours merge everywhere. Red. Orange. Yellow. Green. Blue. Indigo. Violet. Every colour of the rainbow. Every colour is definite and bold.

The sun is a purple-blue disc in the sky. When day arrives, it is immediate, as if a light is switched on and the sun appears in the same place every day. The sky turns white and orange clouds appear and drift lazily by.

When night comes, it is instant. A solitary silver

moon and constellations of bright flickering stars replace the sun.

This is Tropal, the Third Dimension, and something is coming.

Something unwanted.

Something evil.